STEPHEN R. KING

DEMON KEEPERS

Bring your soul closer to heaven or hell. Climb past the emotions to pull yourself up to safety. Where is the whisper in the darkness coming from? Discover every fear while you read four new horror adventures and the tales of DEMON KEEPERS.

Copyright © 2023 by Stephen R. King

This book is a work of fiction. Any references to historical events, real people, or real places are used fictitiously. Other names, characters, places, and events are products of the author's imagination, and any resemblance to actual events or places or person, living or dead, is entirely coincidental.

All rights reserved, including the right to reproduce this book or portions thereof in any form whatsoever.

Manufactured in the United States of America
Designed by Magic Pen Designs

CONTENTS

DEMON KEEPERS....4

THE CAMP....50

DESPERATE TIMES...89

BEAR HUNT....130

DEMON KEEPERS

"Honestly, Calvin, how do you expect to remain employed when you have such deplorable skills? How did you even end up in this line of work? How have you not been fired outright? I'm sure even the Vatican has an HR department that could dispose of trash like you before lunchtime."

Father Calvin Berkeley made no verbal reply. He only appeared to read and pray. This attack on his person was somewhat new but not altogether surprising. His adversaries were not all relics of the past, as Hollywood would like people to think. Sometimes, Calvin just had to brace himself for brutal attacks from his own dead mother.

"You look like a jackass, for one thing. And then you come in here and smell like breakfast at the retirement home. There's no charm at all. You just suck."

At this insult, Calvin almost snorted with laughter, but he managed to hold it together.

The victim today was a young man, about fourteen. His black hair was greasy and unwashed, and his brown eyes looked almost red in the light. Once clear and unblemished according to his mother, the skin on his face was now littered with scars of varying sizes—and they were all self-inflicted. He had first manifested symptoms a few weeks prior, when he cut into the family dog with a steak knife and declared the Jack Russell Terrier to be perfectly rare. Things only went downhill from there.

Calvin had been called in a little late, typical of the church, but he had come to expect as much. It was alright with him; he no longer had a great interest in saving the hosts, he only wished to arrive before the inhabitants got bored and jumped to another vessel. Or disappeared altogether, only to show up in some other time zone— or on some other continent and in some new and terribly afflicted body.

Calvin stifled most of his amusement but allowed himself a light chuckle as he told the boy, "Alright, alright. I know I suck. No need to rub it in. But why don't we get to the important part here? Eh? I'm bored, and so are you, so why drag this out?"

The boy's eyes widened. He showed his teeth and stretched his lips into such a snarl that his gums showed a deep red. Calvin imagined that the boy, in other times, was a favorite of his dentist. It looked like he flossed well and stayed away from sugary snacks and sodas. Of course, Calvin realized, this might mean that he was actually one of his dentist's *least* favorite patients, depending on the good doctor's motivations with regard to his vocation.

The same went for Calvin and others of his ilk. Many were good practitioners, individuals who really wanted the outcome to benefit the victim, or patient, or what-have-you. These were the old originals, the ones who kept their collars starched and their waters holy. They were the true believers, and Calvin had to imagine that their hearts were as pure as the driven snow.

He both hated and pitied that type of priest.

Calvin was not one to put his life on the line for some weak soul that allowed their vice and ignorance to drag them so far to the other side of morality that someone had to be paid to come in and drag them back to the land of the living.

No, for Calvin, the job of exorcism was no different than that of the paramedic who pumped NARCAN into the veins of another overdose victim.

Well...it wasn't completely the same. Because, after all, what did the paramedic glean from the experience of saving a junkie, besides the chance to do it all over again? No, Calvin had benefits, and he exercised them well. These benefits were, in fact, his motivation for remaining a part of the Order.

"You can go ahead and get out or not," Calvin said. "But I have a recommendation for you."

He produced a small, gleaming box from his inside coat pocket. Calvin always wore a leather jacket over his wrinkled shirt and collar. The overcoats of the old priests were so unwieldy, and they lacked a particular style. Calvin had long ago forsaken the uniform of the pious; he yearned to be as bad as he felt— as bad as they had *made him* feel. So, he dressed in a way that, he hoped, broadcasted his lack of allegiance to the norm.

"You…it's Gazali, if I am not mistaken? You don't want to just go bouncing out of this kid as soon as I make you do it. Trust me. I've spent the weekend in this house, and there is *nothing* here that I would want to get inside of, if you know what I mean."

At this, Calvin winked at the boy, or rather, at the thing inside of the boy.

"Wha…what kind of trick is this, priest?" said a voice that belonged not to the boy, but to the entity that had assumed control of his functions. "Your duty is to banish me back to hell, not give me a vessel, or to recommend one."

"Let my duty be my own damn business," Calvin said. "I'm not giving you passage back to hell, you hear me? No rites, no prayers, no ritual. If you want out of this bedroom, you get in this box. If you want to stay in here with the model airplanes and crusty socks and this kid's mother constantly spilling soup and tears all over the place, then you go right ahead. I'm out of here."

Calvin got up and headed for the door, snapping the little box closed and putting it back into his pocket. He stooped to take up his satchel before he left.

"Wait!" a deep and hissing voice shouted from within the boy. "Don't go all at once! It is so terribly boring here! You are the only fun I've had since I found this host!"

Calvin stopped, his hand on the knob.

"I know," he said over his shoulder. "But that doesn't mean that I have to stay and entertain you. There are a lot of other things that I would rather be doing."

He opened the door and stepped out into the hallway. It was fifteen degrees warmer outside of the room. Calvin shook off the cold and reached back to close the door.

"No! Please wait! You must! I beg you!"

Calvin paused with his hand still on the doorknob.

"You beg me?" he repeated to the body on the bed.

The boy's eyes were full of fear, and his chest moved up and down with heaving breaths. In the moment, it was difficult for Calvin to tell if the child was spilling through— if it were a moment where the veil between the physical and spiritual worlds became thin, and the victim of possession was almost able to communicate, in spite of the demonic presence within them.

"Please. I cannot stay here any longer. Let me out," the voice said.

"Getting out means getting in the box, is that clear?" Calvin replied.

"Yes, yes. Whatever you say, just free me from this terrible place. I will escape soon enough, you know."

Calvin chuckled as he reentered the room. He closed and locked the door once again. Once he had set down his bag, he again withdrew the small box from his pocket. The box was wooden, polished to a high shine. It had no lock or latch, only simple hinges. What the demon did not know, could now know, was that the symbols carved into the inside of the box were more effective than any lock when it came to imprisoning the ancient forces of hell.

"Alright, come on. I haven't got all day," Calvin said, holding the box out toward the boy on the bed.

The child seemed to swell and deflate, as if the presence inside of him had gathered its belongings all together before taking leave. The room grew colder yet; frost formed on the windows and coated the mirror over the dresser. The air seemed to vibrate.

Calvin felt his fingers freeze, and the box took on a weight that was not physical but nonetheless made his arm weary as he struggled to hold it still. Finally, when he snapped the lid shut with his thumb, the temperature in the room returned to normal. The air seemed to stabilize, and it was again possible to draw a breath without feeling like some terrible poison was being drawn into the lungs.

The boy stirred, sniffled, and began to whimper. He touched his scarred face with trembling hands, as if he needed to feel them to make sure it was real. His brown eyes lacked the sinister sheen from before. Instead, they shimmered with unshed tears. Calvin went to the door and called for the mother. When she came rushing into the room, she took one look at her son and collapsed on the bed, taking him into her arms and weeping. She thanked Calvin over and over again through her tears. He said nothing, only nodded and waved her off. Her check was already in his pocket— he required payment up front because it allowed him to get out of the house and away from these gratuitous displays of relief and affection.

But it wasn't that check he had come for in the first place, and it wasn't any sort of religious propriety either. Calvin's real reward was in the little wooden box that he had tucked into the inside pocket of his leather jacket. The box that now buzzed and roiled with such malevolence that he could feel it against his chest.

"Be calm, my friend," he whispered as he went down the stairs and headed for the front door. Above him, he could still hear the mother crying. She had now begun to sing praises to heaven. He figured this was all for the better, that someone up there might appreciate her enthusiasm.

"I think you will be quite comfortable in the place where I am taking you," he said. "And I can promise that you won't be lonesome."

****

When Calvin was just out of the seminary, he had been radicalized— so to speak.

The church does not train its young priests to exorcise demons since it is a particular and delicate devotion, something that is approached with much prayer and deliberation. Generally, it is only men of the cloth who have spent a lot of time in foreign parishes who are even considered for the rite, being that these priests often see far more demonic activity in the wilds of the third world than an average priest can expect to in Boston or San Antonio.

Calvin never went abroad, and he had no real desire to serve the less fortunate in the ghettos of his homeland, but he did have a particularly large chip on his shoulder the moment when fate decided to make him an exorcist.

His path through the seminary was bleak, humiliating, and marked by a myriad of abuses. He had only found his way into the calling because— as his probation officer had told him as a sixteen-year-old orphan with two strikes— it was either that or juvenile detention, and eventually prison, at the rate he was going.

As it turned out, seminary did, indeed, keep Calvin out of prison. It did not, however, shelter him from violence.

Late in the evenings, after the meal was finished and the dormitories were tidied, quiet with the sleeping sounds of so many innocent souls, Father Carnahan would come calling. Carnahan knew that Calvin was on thin ice, and he would make all manner of promises and threats, and he would play Calvin's own troubled past against him in order to get what he wanted from the boy.

The things that happened in those late nights were not recorded anywhere— not even in Calvin's memory. He had erased all of it, relegated it to the realm of the unproven. These were things that happened to someone else, somewhere else, someplace where justice did not exist, and young voices did not matter. That was not a place where Calvin wanted to live, so he decided that, in order to continue living, he must make himself understand that his memory was unreliable, and he managed to forget everything.

Everything, that is, except the anger.

When Calvin graduated from the seminary and accepted a position in a small parish in Asheville, North Carolina, he was a young man filled with knowledge and hatred in equal measures. He did not desire to save souls or feed the hungry, but he knew he needed to feed himself, to maintain shelter in a cold world, and now he had a vocation. Calvin practiced the faith as one might wield a shovel or a wrench: it was a tool that was useful for making a living.

For some time, he eked out a living in the hills of North Carolina, tending to his small flock as little as possible and generally just trying to stay out of the way. He liked to read, and he liked to drink scotch, so he indulged in those passions as much as possible. Sunday mornings, he would sober up and emerge from his study for long enough to deliver some shallow and thoughtless message at mass, his sermons as wholesome and thoughtful as reheated leftovers.

Calvin might have been content to live out his days in such a cycle— he was never hungry, he had a roof over his head, the police didn't see the need to hassle him for the first time in his life. But then, something happened that opened his eyes to an entirely different realm of possibility, a life that could be led in order to exact vengeance on those who had wronged him.

It had been late on a Friday night, and Calvin was somewhat drunk and very involved in a volume of Faulkner. His study at the rectory was dark, kept that way by the thick curtains that he made sure were always closed. He sat with his feet propped up on an ottoman, a whorl of cigarette smoke moving slowly around his head. The meager light from a single dim lamp was all he needed to read by. His whiskey glass was close by his ever-ready hand.

Someone knocked at the door to the outside. Softly, tentatively. Calvin ignored it. Sometimes, drifters or bums would come by the rectory looking for a handout. If there were any nuns about, they would usually scrounge something up for the poor souls, but Calvin kept out of that end of the business.

They knocked again, more insistently this time, and Calvin could hear hushed voices through the wooden door. When they knocked a third time, he cursed and dropped his booted feet to the floor, mashing out his cigarette in an ashtray before flinging the door open.

"What do you want?" he snapped.

The night was windy and quite cold for North Carolina, and the two figures in the doorway shivered and stamped their feet. The dim light from the study made their eyes glow, and Calvin could see that it was a man and a woman, weary, maybe frightened, but clean and warmly dressed. Not bums or transients. They didn't even look like hippies from the mission; these were hill folk, and they must have come with a purpose.

"We's lookin for a priest," the man said, pointing to the collar at Calvin's neck. "We's lookin for you."

Calvin had hesitated, prepared to tell them to move along, that there was nothing he could do for them at that hour, not for whatever it was they had expected in coming. But he stopped, noticing a broken and desperate look in the woman's eyes. She was probably in her early forties, some years younger than the man, though they seemed to be a couple. Her hair was lank and pale, and her eyes were glassy, dark-rimmed with fatigue, but they burned with a light that belied a passionate soul.

He invited them to step inside without really realizing that he was doing it, and soon, they sat before him in the study, the man smoking a cigarette he had cadged from Calvin, the woman hugging herself as though she were still cold, despite the warmth of the room.

"We are not what you might call religious folks," she said. "But we have come to an impasse. We are being tormented by something that is not of this world. If a man of the cloth can't help us, I will have to suppose that we're doomed."

Calvin noted that she spoke in the vernacular of an educated hillbilly while her husband used a less ceremonious manner of speech. Calvin directed his reply to the woman.

"I want to tell you a secret, Ms.—"

"Peach," she said. "I'm Vera Peach, and this is my common-law husband, Virgil."

"Mrs. Peach," Calvin went on, "I want to tell you a secret, one that no one else in this town knows, and one that I wish to continue being a secret, but I think it best that you know where we stand. I, too, am not what one might call religious. Your poor luck has brought you down from your home and led you to the door of the one priest in the country who probably prays to God less than you do. I am very sorry, but whatever other-worldly nemesis it is that you believe you are facing is well outside of my level of expertise, not to mention my pay grade."

Vera Peach bowed her head in a gesture that might have seemed like prayer if she were not cursing under her breath. Virgil looked from his wife to the faithless priest and back again. The room was beginning to feel very small.

"Listen, Mister," Virgil said. "I don't really give two damns what you believe or don't believe. You got a responsibility to people, whether you like it or not. That collar on your neck is supposed to mean something. We've got a problem with my wife's sister, and it's not something any doctor can fix."

Calvin sat forward, considered his drink, tried to think of a way to get these people out of his study without causing more trouble. But there was something about the tone of Virgil's voice and his choice of words that stirred a morbid curiosity within him.

"I think you could help us, whether you believe it or not," Virgil went on. "You've got your robes and your fancy words; and me, well I've got traps."

"Traps?" Calvin asked. "You mean, like, animal traps?"

Virgil only nodded, a gleam of pride and confidence in his eyes, and he blinked against the smoke from his cigarette.

Calvin went on. "And you think that these animal traps would be helpful to me in dealing with your sister-in-law?"

"Sister-in-common-law is what I've taken to calling her, but yeah. Trust me, Father, you don't want to tangle with Sally these days unless she's standing in the middle of a trapline. Otherwise, she'll make a mess of your face, your hands, whatever she can get hold of."

Calvin could scarcely believe the conversation he was having. He looked around his little study. He looked at the books and the carved oak desk, the flickering light from the fireplace. He looked at the windows with their wreaths of frost. He'd had no intention of going out into that cold night, but the words and the eyes of his visitors had stimulated a curiosity in him that he could not ignore.

"Well, I cannot promise you that my visit will be of any benefit to you or your sister," he said, speaking again to Vera Peach. "In fact, I would advise against any measure of optimism. However, I will consent to come out to your place and see the poor woman, if only to ascertain if she might be in need of any serious medical help."

Vera and Virgil looked at one another in the yellow light of the study. His look seemed to say "I told you so," but so did hers.

"She's beyond medical help, Father," Vera said. "You'll understand what I mean soon enough."

****

The trek had taken less time than Calvin expected. Through the cold and windy dark, he had followed Vera Peach and Virgil— whose last name he never learned and thus assumed was inconsequential— into the foothills that bordered the edge of town.

He didn't know Vera and Virgil at all, had not even seen them in the town, but he was very familiar with their type. Many people came down from the hills when the time was right. Some came to barter and trade, others brought crops or handmade goods to sell. In the peak of summer, when the town was teeming with tourists either passing through or enjoying the peace and quiet that the town offered, a steady flow of hill folk came into town every day. These folks set up stands on sidewalks and laid out their wares on woven blankets.

As such, Calvin knew the attitudes of the hill folk well. He knew that they were a self-sufficient lot, hardworking and creative. They were also private, prideful, and could be stern. Above all other things, these people were fearless. As he walked up into the dark and frosty highlands behind two strangers, he decided that this was why he consented to go along. He saw fear in the eyes of people who feared nothing, and he wanted desperately to witness what it was that had struck such anxiety in their hearts.

They made good time as they climbed the slow rise into a dark holler over the town. Calvin kept up but gasped and coughed and cursed himself for being so out of shape. Vera and Virgil were unfazed by the exertion and didn't seem to notice that their guest was struggling, so he made even more effort to appear unaffected.

In time, they came through a patch of briar and into a clearing that contained a handsome, white house of hewn timber, as well as a surprisingly large barn set back behind the house. The house was dark, as was the barn, but there came from the barn the sound of a horse whinnying in great protest.

"Come and see my sister," Vera said. "Her name is Katherine."

Calvin began to walk toward the house, but Vera reached out and caught him by the elbow. When he looked at her, she motioned toward the barn, where the terrible horse was screaming and kicking as though it were trying to escape from a swarm of wasps. Calvin could not see the horse, but he heard the wooden sides of the old barn reverberate under the swift strikes of rock-hard hooves, and he could hear the beast crying out wildly.

"She's out here," Vera said.

"It's safer," Virgil said.

Calvin asked, "Safer for whom?"

His hosts only trudged on toward the barn with grim determination as Virgil answered, "For everyone."

Virgil pulled aside one of the barn's big, sliding doors, and they entered into the light of a single lantern. The floor was dirt, swept smooth and scattered with bits of animal feed and clumps of straw. There seemed to be no movement besides the frenzied action of the horse, which threw wild bands of darkness against the wooden walls, making the entire barn some sort of awful shadowbox play.

Vera and Virgil urged Calvin on ahead, between the empty stalls, though they now seemed timid, less eager to reach the objective of their mission. Vera had taken to muttering to herself, though Calvin detected no profanity now that they were in the presence of the problem. Virgil walked about two steps behind Calvin, as though to prevent him from fleeing— or to better use him as a shield against whatever evil lurked on the other side of the barn.

When Calvin finally stepped into the circle of light that shone from the lantern that he could now see was hanging from a low rafter in the center of the barn, he was shocked to realize that there was no mad horse being housed in the stables. The screams, the kicks, the snorts, all came from the slight and bedraggled human form that was chained in the stall beneath the light.

It was a woman, probably in her late twenties or early thirties. Calvin found himself wondering if Vera was, in fact, quite a bit younger than she looked. Perhaps she had been aged by the strain of seeing her sister become what she was now, which was something frightening and other-worldly.

The woman thrashed about on all fours. Her fingers, blackened with earth and grime and animal feces, dug into the dirt floor like claws, and she snatched and pawed as though she might dig her way out of the stall. In this endeavor, she would be unsuccessful either way, for someone had fitted a leather collar around her neck. The collar was attached to a chain, which, in turn, was attached to a heavy ring anchored in the wooden wall of the stall.

"You chained her?" Calvin asked, incredulity mixing with fear in his voice.

"Had to," Virgil nodded. "She kept chewing through the ropes."

At the sound of their voices, the woman ceased her thrashing and writhing, snapping her head around to look at them. Her wild, dark-rimmed eyes focused on Calvin, and she smiled a slow, broad smile. He could feel her gaze settling on the collar around his neck, and he could imagine her squeezing it with her filthy hands. His voice came in short gasps as she cocked her head to one side and then the other. She stood more than ten feet away from Calvin, on the other side of a locked, steel gate, her hair ratty and wild in the yellow light of the lantern, but he could feel a presence much closer, sizing him up, mocking him, breathing fetid breath into his face.

"Oh, look," the woman said. "Sissy went and fetched a preacher man."

The voice that came from her mouth was incongruent with the frame and the face, though the demented depth of hatred in her eyes seemed to match the venom in that husky tone. Calvin blinked hard and forced himself to take a deep breath and ignore the unmistakable scent of death that threatened to close in on him.

"I am a priest, actually," he replied. "Though, I am sure you know that."

Impossibly, the smile widened, and Calvin thought that the poor woman's face might actually split. The body strained casually at the chain around her neck, and she released a strangled laugh.

"Oh, yes, I know a great many things, Father Berkely," she rasped.

Calvin felt a finger of cold fear run down the middle of his spine. He had not spoken his name. He had not even given his last name to Vera and Virgil. It was not listed in the church directory or printed on the door of his study. He introduced himself to everyone as Father Calvin; leaving off his last name gave him a sense of privacy that he treasured, but this stranger had spoken his name as though they were old acquaintances, though certainly not of the friendly variety.

Calvin smoothed the front of his shirt, adjusted his coat, stalling for time while he considered his situation. There was certainly something unnatural afoot, and the church would never sanction him having gone even this far, but he was seldom concerned with the rules and regulations of the Roman Catholic Church.

"And what is your name?" he finally asked.

Vera spoke from somewhere behind him: "Gretchen. Her name is Gretchen."

Calvin glanced back at her and tried to look casual. She was half-hidden in shadow, and she clutched a pitchfork. He heard a slight metallic rattling and noticed that Virgil was busy setting what looked like a fox trap.

"Thank you, Vera," Calvin said. "But that is not what I was asking."

He tuned back to the woman locked in the stall.

"What I want to know is, what is *your* name?"

The eyes narrowed to slits, and there was a growling sound from somewhere deep within the woman's body. She was no longer smiling but had her lips curled in a sneer of derision. The lantern flickered, though there was no breeze in the barn, only cold, still air, charged with hate and fear.

"I have been called many things over the millennia," the voice said. "But my proper name is Agrogaut."

"Ah, that's a lovely name," Calvin replied, which caused the woman's body to strain toward him with renewed fervor, the chain coming taut and her eyes bulging in a red and trembling face.

"You have no business here, Father Berkely!" the voice shouted. "This woman is mine to do with as I please. You have no power over me. I can sense your faith and your fear. One is weak, and the other is your weakness!"

He reached into his coat and removed a small, glass bottle with a cork stopper. He removed the cork and held the bottle up to the light. It was half-full of clear fluid.

"My faith is not in question here," he lied, "The church is taking a new approach to nuisances such as yourself, Agrogaut. You see, they found that they were losing too many great orators to the order of exorcism, and of course, after a time in the field, those men were wasted."

The eyes followed the bottle, the body recoiled slightly.

"Exorcists nowadays are more like technicians. We understand the tools of the trade, and we make quick work of pests like you. It is quicker and far less messy. I am surprised you don't know any of this. I'm guessing it has been some time since you've been out and about."

The growling increased in volume, and the woman's body was drawn up as though she were taking the deepest of breaths. The eyes still looked only at the bottle, which Calvin now moved to sit on the top of a post, just beyond the reach of the chained body.

Calvin had sensed that night that this would be the moment that everything changed for him. He was well outside the bounds of accepted reality, as well as beyond the reach of what he was trained and approved to do. If he left the barn in one piece, he would do so as either an exorcist of his own design or as a former priest, no longer permitted to wear the collar, banished from all positions within the parish.

When he threw the steel trap, doused with holy water, into the stall and heard the screams of agony and blasphemy that erupted from within, he knew he had his answer. Agrogaut left the farm in the hills contained within an old cigar box, inscribed with the names of God in ballpoint pen. Vera and Virgil said they would tend to Gretchen's wounds, thankful that she was now only afflicted by wounds of the flesh and had been freed from the torment of her spirit.

They were unable to pay him for his services, and Calvin would not have accepted anything if they had offered. What he came away with that night was a knowledge so profound, so unthinkable that he knew it was worth more than any sum of money. He had bluffed and won; faith was not necessary in order to command the forces of evil. It was Agrogaut's belief in the systems of power, along with some good old-fashioned element of surprise, that enabled Calvin to cast the demon out.

Back in his study, as the cold outside settled in on a moonless night and drew frost pictures on the window panes, he poured another glass of whiskey and sat watching the cigar box that practically vibrated with rage on the top of his desk.

****

Calvin had come a long way from cigar boxes and animal traps, but the basic idea had remained the same. There had to be a blessed element, whether it was water or a crucifix or a reputable relic. Once, he had utilized a bit of cloth that was rumored to have been touched by a saint— which saint it was depended on who you asked. At any rate, the cloth had been enough to convince the entity, and that was all that mattered.

Another necessity was some instrument of violence. It didn't have to be a physical weapon; in fact, as in the case of Gazali and the young boy, an unwelcome presence could be enough to convince a demon to move on to other vessels. The boy's mother had been so insistent in her care and worry that Gazali had opted to try his luck in the box, and that is where he would stay until Calvin deigned to free him.

The box itself was the last element in the process. A suitable container had to be put to use. Calvin had been lucky the first time around, as most demons were not likely to be held at bay in a cigar box with some hastily written charms on the lid, but Agrogaut had been one of the old ones, out of practice and practically out of commission. That particular entity was so flustered and flummoxed that they might have been kept in a soda bottle until a more appropriate prison could be contrived.

"Prison" turned out to be quite an accurate description. Much like the brass lamps in the genie tales of old, the boxes, vials, jars, bottles, and tins that lined the shelves of Calvin's current study were impenetrable penitentiaries for the malevolent beings contained inside them. He had, over the years, collected a veritable Legion of entities, labeling each one with its name, a date, and the location of the exorcism. What might look to the casual observer like a wall of curios, a broad shelf of antique containers that might have held sugar, flour, ashes or trinkets, was actually the greatest spiritual weapon ever devised on earth—it just was not fully assembled.

On the back wall of the shelf, Calvin had drawn a large pentagram. This symbology was necessary in containing and restraining the demons, and it also helped to maintain their connections to the underworld. Calvin had discovered, through trial and error, that demons were somewhat like car batteries: if they were left "unhooked" and unused, their power waned, and eventually, they were of no good to anyone. He thought with wonder of the countless demons wasting away in strong holds at the Vatican. Every entity that was cast out and contained by any exorcist besides himself was sent to the Holy city and kept forever in a locked room with no power source for the beings within.

Calvin avoided contributing to this wasteful collection by reporting that all of his exorcisms were merely cast out. He always wrote in his reports that he failed to apprehend the demon, that it slipped away, perhaps leapt into a family pet and scampered out the back door never to be seen again. Meanwhile, each evil presence that he interacted with left with him, in his pocket or his brief case, with promises of a better existence, a future, a greater purpose.

There was another reason for the pentagram behind the shelf, and it was one of classification. At four of the five points of the star, there sat containers that held some of the most impressive and dangerous entities he had encountered in his long career. These demons held positions of honor because they had impressed upon him their pedigrees, their lineage, and their awful deeds. Some of these ones had required him to shed blood, both his own and that of the mortal victims, but he had brought each of them back here, to his home and to which he had come to think of as his armory.

There was still one open spot, at the very top of the pentagram, and it was the filling of this space that Calvin now anticipated to be the pinnacle of his life's work. It was what he thought about every morning when he rose and dreamt of every night when he went to sleep.

Now, as he placed the box containing Gazali into an open space among the dozens of assorted vessels between the points of the star, he thought again about what invisible beast would someday— hopefully soon— occupy the space at the top of the pentagram, and he thought about what he might finally be able to accomplish once this esteemed position was finally filled.

****

Three thousand miles away, in a small town just across the U.S./Mexico border, a group of teenaged kids were loitering by a river. They had cut out of school early, browsed and pranked in the market square, eaten and flirted at an outdoor restaurant on the edge of the town.

The late afternoon found them at the muddy banks, skipping stones and wading in the shallows, the cool water helping them to combat the heat of the day. A young man held the hand of his love. A young woman splashed and laughed in the brown current. Others sat on the banks or climbed around among the shrubby plants and tangled roots of the slope, smoking cigarettes and exchanging gossip. Some kids who had not skipped school came down after the last bell, everyone bringing news of the kinds of things that kids do when they are bored or troubled or in love, no one anxious to go home to their parents and chores and homework.

A boy of about fifteen years climbed to the top of a narrow railroad bridge, walked to the center of the span and stood on the edge with his arms out like the crucified limbs of Christ. The gathered youth on the banks and in the shallows below fell silent, save for one girl that called out for him to not be so stupid. The river was shallow, and the bridge was too high.

Pride or stupidity plugged the boy's ears, and he jumped, lowering his arms and plunging like a nail into the turbulent waters. He stayed down for some time. Too long.

Shortly, there were other boys and girls crashing through the current to the area where the boy had disappeared. Voices became frantic as the afternoon quickly turned from relaxed to panicked and began to turn the corner into tragic.

And then, he reappeared, some yards downstream. His arms were cut, his face bloodied and quickly obscured by a crimson flow from a bad gash over his eye, but he was conscious and standing upright in waist-high waters. No one could imagine how he had drifted past the search party, how he had come up on his own given the injuries he sustained.

As they rushed to help him and bind his wounds in their shed t-shirts and handkerchiefs, the boy only wandered absently to the river's edge and knelt down, his eyes open and bright but seemingly blind to all of his friends and classmates. Where he squatted in the mud, he began to draw on the ground with the tip of his finger. He drew symbols that meant nothing to anyone but him, strands of letters and other things that looked like broken letters, small pictures, dots and dashes, whorls and swirls, and crosshatchings.

The boy was so intent on drawing his nonsensical masterpiece that he did not hear his friends talking to him, asking him how he felt and if he needed help walking home. He did not notice when the sky grew dark, and he gave no reaction when huge drops began to fall from the sky. One by one, his friends left him until there was only one that remained. She was his closest confidant and oldest friend. They each had a secret crush, one loving the other behind their friendly smiles and gestures, neither willing to admit their true feelings.

As she watched him in his absolute focus, blood still running from his wounds, the caked residue again turned to fluid by the falling rain, she had the sensation that she was watching a stranger. He did not acknowledge her, just as he did not acknowledge the rain or the wind or the growing cold. He made no sounds save for the occasional mumble or whispered word, nothing that she could distinguish or reply to.

Finally, she went to his house and returned with the boy's grandmother. The old woman had wrapped herself up into a length of thick, woven material and covered her head against the rain. When she arrived and saw the state of her grandson, knelt and looked into his wide and expressionless eyes, the old woman began to weep, and she pressed her head firmly into the wet earth as a fervent prayer began to emit from her lips.

The boy snarled and moved away, clambering over the bank like a hermit crab, bent and agile and quick. As the girl looked on, the grandmother continued to pray, and the boy continued to try and write his unending spell in the mud, rain washing away each symbol as soon as he scrawled it into the earth.

The prayers and pleadings of the grandmother seemed to anger the boy, who continually lumbered away to further and flatter spaces but could apparently not stop the boundless range of his grandmother's supplications. Soon, his head snapped back, and he emitted a howl that rose above the wind and rain and raised goosebumps along the girl's arms. Before she knew what he was doing, the boy took up a flat rock from the riverbank, the size of a dinner plate, and he rushed at his own poor grandmother with the rock raised above his head and a wicked, unconstrained look in his eyes.

When he brought the stone down upon the old woman's

gray head, there was a dull, wet sound and only thy softest grunt. Her blood ran in small streams down the bank, red and somehow lovely against the dark mud. It mingled with the river waters and disappeared in the rapid current.

The girl ran. The boy returned to his drawings and mumblings, crouching right next to his murdered grandmother, the person who had raised him since birth.

At the Arch Diocese in Boston, Father Leonard Carnahan leafed through a sheaf of papers and shook his head.

"Calvin lost another one, I see," the Father said to his companion on the other side of the mahogany desk.

The office was large, lavish, and lit by green lamps on the desk on tables on either side of a brown, leather sofa. The shelves along one wall reached to the ceiling and contained countless dusty tomes, the titles on their spines worn and obscured by generations of reverent hands.

"I can't remember the last time he sent a subject to the Vatican," the other priest said. "He's good at casting them out, but he has a slippery time after that."

Carnahan grunted.

"There is much that is slippery about Father Calvin Berkely," he muttered. "You can take my word for that."

The other priest did not make a reply but nodded as he read the report. His name was Father Hinkley, and he had a youthful face and short, red hair. His pale hands were freckled on the backs and trembled ever so slightly as he read.

"He is scarcely ordained to be performing such rites, am I correct?" Hinckley said. "Yet, it seems to me that he is the most active exorcist in the church."

Carnahan leaned back in his chair and webbed his fingers behind his gray head. His stomach stretched the seams of his black shirt.

"Everything you say is correct, my friend," he said. "Calvin is always one mistake away from being stripped of all titles, and he does not care one bit. His methods are unorthodox and his motives shadowed and impure. I refuse to believe that he loses every demon into the ether...I'm not even sure if he is engaging with legitimate cases of possession. He operates outside of the normal parameters of the church, and he does not always receive permission through the proper channels."

Father Hinkley's fair eyebrows arched. "Then why is he allowed to continue?"

Father Carnahan sighed. It was a rumbling, grumbling sound from somewhere deep in his chest. His deep-set eyes took on a darkness that surpassed the shadowed atmosphere of the study.

"The powers-that-be, crooked politicians that they are, have deemed him effective. They say he is popular among the flocks, being that they think he has set them free from so many instances of demonic affliction. Simply put: to do away with Calvin would be bad press."

Father Hinkley laid the reports back down on the desk and picked up a steaming mug of coffee. He was a teetotaler, a man of great caution and a calm nature. Carnahan, conversely, had a weakness for the simple pleasures of the flesh. For his part, Carnahan sipped on a tumbler of twelve-year Scotch and rubbed his temple with thick fingers.

"Well, maybe they are right," Hinkley offered. "The church has had plenty of negative press in recent years. I suppose it would be foolish of us to turn our backs on anyone that improves our image in the eyes of the people."

Carnahan looked up at his peer with brooding eyes. He rotated the rocks glass in his hands, balanced between the tips of his fingers. He said nothing.

"After all," Hinkley continued, "Couldn't anything that brings people closer to the Lord, anything that inspires wonder and reverence of the mercy of our heavenly Father, be considered the work of Heaven itself?"

At this, Carnahan scoffed.

"Father Hinkley, you are a good man and a respectable priest, but you are young and naive. I can assure you that there is nothing noble or pious about the works of Calvin Berkeley. His is an opportunist and a slanderer. There is nothing that man does that is not intended to further his own corrupt agenda."

There was a timid knock at the study door. Carnahan called for the visitor to enter, and a boy of about thirteen entered, his eyes cast to the floor.

Carnahan turned to look at a clock on the wall.

"Ah, yes, I nearly forgot. We have a lesson this afternoon. Father Hinkley, I am sure you will not mind if we take up this discussion at another time?"

The younger priest rose and began to gather his things.

"Of course not. I have business to attend to myself. It's been a pleasure visiting with you, Father Carnahan, and thank you for the coffee."

As he was leaving, Father Hinkley tried to smile at the boy, but he seemed as though his mind was somewhere else, and he made no eye contact.

****

The call came in the middle of the night, as they always seemed to. This did not bother Calvin that much— he was a night owl, anyway. He had long considered the harsh light of morning to be anathema and morning people to be among the more demented in society. He was partial to sitting up until just before dawn, lost in his books and his compulsive smoking, nursing glass after glass of whisky until the words on the pages before him began to blur and sleep came to claim him in spite of his valiant protests.

So, it was that routine he was partaking in when Calvin came to receive the phone call from Chamizal. The voice on the other end was male, weary and afraid, spoke halting but altogether decent English. Over the course of several minutes, Calvin was able to gather that there had been an incident in a small, border town, that there was evidence of demonic activity, and that a teenage boy was exhibiting some exceptional symptoms of possession.

"I can sympathize with you, Mr. Perrera," Calvin said. "I know how frightening and difficult these situations can be. However, I am not sure if you are aware of this, but I am on the east coast of the United States. Given the apparent severity of your nephew's condition, I might as well be on the moon. I am sure that there is someone closer to your proximity who can try to help you."

There was a short pause, silence on the other end of the line. Then, Perrara replied.

"Yes, Mr. Calvin, we have had two priests here already. One from the local parish, and another came from Matamoros. Both were...unsuccessful."

Calvin sipped his drink. His feet were up on a leather ottoman, and the room was warm and comfortable. Something about the night reminded him of that night so long ago in Asheville, when Vera and Virgil came to coax him out of his cozy study and changed his life forever. Something about the evening was charged with fate.

"Why do you believe that I would be more successful?" he asked.

Another uncomfortable silence followed. When Perrera spoke again, it was with hesitation. Calvin thought he sounded like he was struggling to find the words in English that might adequately explain the situation.

"Mr. Calvin...this thing that has taken over my nephew's body..."

"Yes, the demon?" Calvin prompted.

"The demon, yes. You see...it asked for you by name."

At eight o'clock the following morning, Calvin boarded a flight to Monterrey. He slept some on the way across the county, the plane flying west into the rising sun and crossing invisible boundaries that caused time to stand still. When they landed for a layover in Salt Lake City, the clock on the wall of the airport claimed that scarcely an hour had passed.

Calvin grabbed a donut and a hot tea on the way to his next gate. Coffee sounded good, but he wanted to grab some more shut eye on the next leg of the trip. He did not know what manner of challenge might lay ahead of him, and there was no telling how many wakeful hours he would have to spend locked in a battle of wits with the wrathful entity, so he wanted to rest up as much as possible before the plane touched down in Mexico.

At Monterrey, customs checked his passport, gave his luggage a cursory search, and then shepherded him through the gates into the arrivals terminal where he was met by a short, Mexican man with a thick mustache and a broad, white Stetson hat.

"Mr. Perrera, I presume?"

"Father Calvin, I cannot thank you enough for coming so quickly. I hope that you had a pleasant flight."

"Hardly remember a minute of it. And please, just call me Calvin."

"I will, if you agree to call me Joe."

Joe helped Calvin with his bags and led him to a battered, green pickup truck outside. The air was stifling, heat waves lifted from the asphalt of the parking lot and bent the light, making everything low to the ground look as if it were either swimming or melting, Calvin could not decide which.

The pickup truck had no air conditioning, so Calvin was thankful when Joe navigated them away from the airport and onto the open highway. The windows were down, and the wind rushed through the cab of the truck and cooled the air enough to make it tolerable. The wind made for difficult conversation, but Joe was a convivial type, and he did his best to make conversation and apprise his passenger to the state of matter at hand.

"My nephew, Juan, he is in Chamizal, just a few miles down the road. He is being kept at the home of my sister, and I have a room in my house where you can go to rest and store your things while you are here."

"Thank you, that is very gracious of you," Calvin replied, shouting to be heard over the rushing of air. "Where are the boy's parents, if you don't mind me asking?"

Joe's head bobbed up and down, as though he were

agreeing with something that Calvin had said.

"His father took off about the time Juan was born. No one ever heard from him again. His mother, my sister, died of a fever when Juan was still just a little boy. My mother had been taking care of him ever since. That is part of what makes this so difficult…"

Joe trailed off, and Calvin glanced over and saw that the man's cheeks were wet. Joe had described the murder to him over the phone, so he had no real need for more details. He steered the subject away from Joe's dead mother.

"You told me that the entity asked for me by name," he said. "I am curious why it did that. Do you have any idea? Did it say anything about why it wanted me in particular to come here? You see, most demonic entities are loathe to engage with any sort of priest. The whole exorcism thing is not quite like Hollywood would have people believe. A spiritual or physical altercation is a very taxing thing not only for an exorcist but for an entity. Most of them would prefer to remain hidden, and that is why they are so good at mimicking mental illness in the ways that they manipulate their victims. If the presence of a demon remains undetected, then no one ever comes and tries to pry them loose. That is why I find it so strange that you say this one requested a particular exorcist."

Joe reached into the front pocket of his shirt and removed a pack of cigarettes. Relieved, Calvin did the same. The two lit their own, smoked, and rode in silence for a mile or two. Finally, Joe spoke again.

"It is all very confusing," he said. "But when the demon was speaking to the last priest, the one from the parish in Matomoros, that is when your name came up. He…it…said that you were waiting for him, that you had been searching for him."

Calvin sat still and gazed out the window at the brown

countryside. Two small boys were trying to coax a sorry looking burro across a field. The white sun beat down and seemed to turn everything the color of sand.

He had not known, had never known, what entity was destined to take the place at the top of the pentagram, but he had always believed that he would know when he found the one. He had not, however, anticipated that the one might find him.

"Sounds like ramblings," he said to Joe. "Or a trick. These beings, they are craftier than most humans. They can pick up on things that we wouldn't even think of. They are adept at finding a person's weakness, or their greatest fear or regret. A demonic entity will use these personal details to break down a person's defenses, cause doubt, whatever they need to get the upper hand."

Joe shifted in his seat and looked uneasy. They turned onto a dirt road that led through dusty hills and over a bridge that forded a muddy river. Soon, they came into a village of low buildings and humble houses. Kids and dogs played in the narrow streets, and the smoke from a thousand cook fires turned the light a hazy shade of orange.

"I think I know what you speak of," Joe said after a while. "The demon said some things to me as well."

Calvin watched his driver. He could see pain and fear in his eyes, but there was also anger. It was an expression that Calvin was accustomed to seeing on the faces of the parents and family members of the victims he was called in to help.

"It told me that my mother was in hell," Joe said abruptly. "It said that she was suffering in the worst part of hell. That she had led a sinful life and that she would spend an eternity in agony because of it."

Joe's voice was trembling, and he gripped the steering

wheel as if he might float off into nothingness if he let it go.

"Calvin, my mother was the most faithful person I have ever met in my life. She spent more time in prayer than doing anything else, and she gave every spare peso she had to help those less fortunate, and believe me, she did not have much to spare."

Calvin flicked the embers from his smoke and let the butt fall into the dusty street. Small children watched him with wide, dark eyes as they cruised slowly through neighborhoods where the air smelled of frying tortillas and cooking meat.

He hated this part of the job because, in truth, it was the part that made him feel like the biggest hypocrite. His experiences in life had left him with little doubt that no person was good enough or kind enough or generous enough to deserve life after death. He had seen enough evil to know how powerful the forces of hell were. At times like these, he knew what he was expected to say, he just didn't know if he believed any of it.

"Joe, I know I told you that demons can access special knowledge, but they have no business knowing who ends up where after all of this is over," he said. "Whatever it is that is inhabiting your nephew right now was just trying to hurt you, it was trying to get inside your head."

"You know more about what kind of person your mother was then that demon could ever know. If you believe in your heart that she is spending eternity in heaven, then I am certain that is where she is right now. And Joe, I know she is watching over you, and she is proud of you."

Joe's eyes were moist again, and he blinked back tears as he drove. He nodded slightly.

"Yes, yes. Thank you, Father Calvin. I know that what you have said is true."

Calvin leaned back in the seat and watched the little town slide by. Laundry was strung from clotheslines that stretched from house to house. People sold food from roadside stands, and a vendor was carrying an armload of flowers through an intersection.

Ahead, there stood a humble but beautiful mission. The cross that rose from its roof was over thirty feet tall and was adorned with stones that gleamed in the murky light. Garnet and turquoise, bits of chert and marble. The building itself was long and low and mostly open, and Calvin could see people moving about inside the structure. There seemed to be some sort of meal going on, and he realized that he was witnessing the poor feeding the poor. He felt, in the moment, that he might began to weep, just as Joe did.

Perhaps he would stay here. Maybe he would be unable to cast out the demon that tormented the boy and caused him to murder his own beloved grandmother. And if he failed, perhaps he would run off into the desert and forsake his life and his possessions and even his name. He could stay in this place where people took care of one another, where they gave what they had, even when they had so little.

In all of his bitterness and lifelong skepticism, he had never stopped to ask if there might be people somewhere in the world that were, at heart, good. Now, listening to this heartbroken man speak of his dearly departed mother and watching these acts of kindness and charity in a faraway place, a place that felt so little like the home he had always known, he began to doubt his own bitter beliefs.

He wished that he had faith like Joe.

****

Calvin had brought along a curious container. It was a metronome, one of the old, pyramid shaped devices that kept time with an inverted pendulum that ticked back and forth at a rate according to where the weight was adjusted on the pendulum.

This particular metronome was unique for two reasons. The first was that it had a removable back and a hollow interior, so it could be used to store small or shapeless things. The second was that it had belonged to Saint Merrimore of Antigua. The late Saint Merrimore had used the device in countless religious ceremonies and, as such, had had it ornately decorated with all manner of spiritual iconography.

Calvin had come across the metronome at curiosities shop during a trip to New York City. The shop's owner had no idea what he was in possession of, and Calvin walked away with the invaluable object for a paltry few hundred dollars.

It was to be the perfect container for the demon that would complete his collection. The iconography, the symbology, the function, all of it was so perfect, he felt in his blood that this object had found him, rather than him finding it.

With the metronome before him, he now sat at the kitchen table in Joe's sister's home. She was a graceful and quiet woman named Maria, and even through her weariness and fear, Calvin could see that she was a very beautiful woman.

Maria had given him coffee and tamales, and he had eaten slowly and listened to the growls and shrieks, the terrible laughter and horrible curses— in both English and Spanish, as well as some Latin— that came from the next room over. It was the middle of the afternoon, and the kitchen was very hot, but Calvin could feel a draft around his ankles, a subtle gust of cold air that trailed out from underneath the closed and locked door.

He wiped his mouth on a cloth napkin, finished his coffee, and decided that he had waited for long enough when he began to hear his own full name, shouted impatiently from a throat that sounded like it had been gargling broken glass.

"Father Calvin Anthony Berkeley!" the voice croaked. "Father Calvin! Why do you keep me waiting? Finish that slop and come talk to me!"

Joe and Maria looked at Calvin with fearful eyes. He smiled back and made a concerted effort to project an attitude that said this was something he dealt with every day. In a sense, this was true, but it was the first time he had felt himself to be so *in demand* when it came to a demon.

He picked up the key that Maria had set on the table during his lunch and asked: "Shall we?"

He had given specific instructions to both Joe and Maria as to what they were to do in order to assist him during the operation. Joe had referred to the exorcism as a "ceremony," and Calvin had quickly corrected him.

"I am not that kind of exorcist," he said. "This is an operation, or a procedure, if you would prefer. But I do not perform any manner of ceremony and have not for a long time."

Calvin turned the key in the frosted lock and opened the door. He was hit by a soft wall of chilled air, and the sensation would have been wonderful were it not for the horrid smell of death, decay, and human waste. The boy lay tied to the bed with a great many ropes of all thicknesses. New ropes, old ropes, bailing twine, and improvised ropes made from knotted rags. He was so wrapped in ropes that Calvin thought he looked somewhat like a caterpillar that was nearly through building its cocoon. Only his head showed at the top of the mire of ropes.

"He seems secure," Calvin said to Joe, who stood just

behind him.

"Should be," was all Joe replied.

The boy's body stopped struggling and squirming when the eyes fell upon Calvin. There was a peculiar look in those eyes, a mixture of derision and pleasure. Was there relief? Calvin wondered.

Only the slightest smile played across the chapped and bloody lips, and Calvin was glad to not have to witness again the typical demonic grin, the gaping, painful smile that is intended solely to scare the observer and cause pain to the victim. The boy's body seemed calm, the face satisfied.

Calvin stood at the foot of the bed, wondering who would speak first. He had not anticipated that it would be Joe, who suddenly took three quick steps toward the side of the bed and spoke in an angry voice.

"Now you are in for it, you sadistic fu—"

Joe was hurled against the wall by an unseen force. He collided with the plaster and remained held in place, his feet inches from the floor, eyes wide and terrified.

Calvin was impressed. Most demons could manipulate physics and gravity in some small way or another, but to be able to throw a grown man across a room and hold him suspended in the air, while tied to a bed? That was something special.

Calvin looked back and forth between the body in the bed and the man on the wall. Joe seemed to be struggling to breath. Maria stood in the doorway with her eyes closed, silently mouthing a prayer. Calvin was thankful for Maria, who seemed to have a good head on her shoulders.

Instead of admonishing the demon, Calvin walked over and stood in front of Joe, who regarded him with fearful and pleading eyes.

"Now, Joe," he said. "I hope I did not come all this way for you to interrupt my conversation. Did I?"

Joe looked helpless and confused but shook his head as much as he could, which was not much. Calvin caught his eye and gave him a small wink. He still needed Joe on his side, however this played out.

A moment later, Joe was released from his invisible bonds and dropped to the floor where he landed on his hands and knees, gasping for breath like a man who had been sucker punched in the gut.

Calvin turned back to the figure in the bed. It looked malevolently at Joe on the floor, the head turned as far as it could on the pillow.

"So, why don't we stop wasting time?" Calvin said, his voice friendly. "I hear you asked for me by name. Now, while I am flattered, I am also curious. If you know my name, you must also know my track record. You should know that I am very successful at ridding humans of beings such as yourself. That, of course, begs the question: why me? In fact, why any exorcist at all? You clearly have the upper hand here. I know you have bested at least two priests already, and you know that the muckily-mucks in the Arch Diocese are eventually going to send in a ringer. So, what's the rush? Why was it so important for me to travel all the way out here and get you?"

Juan's face assumed a smile that was almost congenial. A small chuckle made the ropes and knots bounce a bit. The voice that came from the boy's mouth was hoarse and ancient but conversational nonetheless.

"Oh, but you see, Father Calvin, it is not this boy or this body that matters. The exorcism is only a matter of formality, which I think should please you. And you will see soon enough that I have no intention of fighting with you. This will be the easiest fee you ever make."

The boy's head turned toward Maria, who was still praying in the doorway, though she now had her eyes open.

"You do have the money for Father Calvin, don't you, foul woman?"

Maria nodded her head stiffly and went on praying. Calvin felt a twist of pain in his stomach.

"You should know," Calvin said, loudly, "that I am not here for money. I am here for you."

It was unclear who Calvin was talking to. He, himself, was not even positive. He had never been in a conversation like this with an entity. The church did, in fact, discourage exorcists from engaging with demons in such a way. But Calvin had never followed the rules, and the things that the demon was saying were interesting.

"I am sure you realize that I still don't understand," Calvin said. "It is unlike you and your type to go willingly, so I am understandably suspicious of your motives."

As he spoke, Calvin removed the metronome from his bag and set it on a table across the room. Juan's eyes followed his movements and settled on the device. There was a brightness in the look that Calvin could not remember ever seeing on the face of the afflicted.

"Is that it?" the voice said. "Is that what I will be traveling in? It is very curious, but I think it shall do just fine. Should we get on with it?"

Calvin paused with his hand still on the metronome. It could not be this easy. It never was. He left the table and stepped close to the bed with authority.

"There will be no exorcism today," he said. "I am not interested in tricks or games. If you want to play with someone, I am sure the local parish will send over another poor sap for you to torment. I am going now."

Calvin began to gather his things. He saw Maria give him a frantic look. Joe moaned from where he still lay on the bedroom floor. Juan's lip curled with spite, but there was a look of desperation in the eyes.

"No! You do not understand!" the voice barked. "I want to go with you. I have been told about you. I am the one you need."

Calvin stopped what he was doing and glanced quickly at Maria. She had her hand over her mouth and her eyes shut tightly. It was hard to tell if she had even registered what the voice had said. Joe was curled on the floor, saying nothing.

"What need could I have of you, anyway?" Calvin asked. "Tell me, what is your name?

There was a silence, and the room seemed to cool a few more degrees. The boy's body tensed, the abdomen swelling with effort. Impossibly, he began to rise from the bed as though he were doing a sit-up. The ropes creaked and groaned and finally snapped, one by one, and the boy came up effortlessly and with a look of triumph on his mild features.

When the voice spoke again, it was with a tone of confident superiority. Despite the heat that cursed everything outside of the room, the boy's breath hung in gusts of fog that accompanied each spoken word.

"I am the one who will become. I am beast and destroyer. I have never inhabited a human form before now. It is only because of your mission and your fury that I have been ordered to come to you, that you might complete the destruction of the church. I am Behemoth."

Calvin did not move, did not speak, for several long breaths. If the demon was not being deceitful, he was in conversation with one of the most infamous demons of the scriptures. Behemoth was to take center stage in the End Times— a period the Calvin had long discounted as a spiritual superstition. But here, just in front of him, he had an entity that claimed to be the beast, the mighty, awful power, and the bringer of all misery.

This was beyond Calvin's wildest dreams. He had a space atop the pentagram that he had reserved for some wicked force, and now, a demon claiming to be a prince was offering its capture and servitude.

He decided in that moment that he would accept no payment from Joe and Maria. He also realized that it was dangerous to continue this conversation in front of them. Joe had risen to his knees but kept his eyes downturned, his head bowed. Maria still stood in the doorway with her lips moving in silent prayer. They seemed to be altogether separate from what was happening in the room, but he knew that they must be listening carefully, hanging on every word. It would not do to have two of the faithful being aware of his plans, vague as they were.

"If you are who you say you are," Calvin said. "Then you certainly have no business here. Be gone!"

Juan's eyes narrowed, and a smile played again at his parched lips.

"Better make it good," said the voice, but Calvin felt it more than heard it. He realized that the Behemoth was speaking to his mind, and the thought chilled him to the bone.

Nonetheless, the demon was right. He could not break

from his usual practices, it could not look easy, or Joe and Maria might speak of it and start rumors that could be problematic.

"I said be gone!" Calvin repeated, shouting this time.

As he spoke, he removed a bottle of holy water from his pocket and threw it hard at the wall above Juan's head. The bottle shattered and rained down shards of glass and a spray of water all over the boy's head and shoulders.

"That is a little better," said the voice in his head.

In a rage that was only partly an act, Calvin grasped the metronome and rushed at the bed. He seized the back of Juan's head with one hand and pressed the metronome against his face with the other.

The voice laughed, audibly now, as Calvin crushed the edges of the pyramid shaped device and the cheek bone of the hapless boy.

"Get out! You beast! This boy is not yours! No! You are mine! Do you hear me? *You are mine!*"

There was a chuckle, a shudder, and the boy went limp. In his mind, Calvin felt as though the demon had winked at him before he went willingly into the metronome. He could not have described how he felt in that moment. He was thrilled and exhilarated, the consequences of this moment meant so much, but he was also nauseous, anxious, and ill-at-ease.

Calvin fixed the cover back to the face of the metronome with shaking hands and stowed the device away into his duffel bag. He could swear that, even with the box closed and zipped into the bag, he could hear it begin to tick, to keep some measure of time determined by the awful entity inside of it. He told himself that it had to be his imagination playing tricks on him. The room was hot again, and he was sweating profusely.

The boy was half-asleep, exhausted and whimpering, as his aunt attended to him with hugs and kisses, tried to get him to drink some water, asked if he would eat something.

"Let him rest for a couple of days," Calvin said as he took up his bag. "He is going to feel like he was in a bad car accident, but he should make a full recovery."

Joe had finally gotten himself up from the floor and was shaking Calvin's hand with cautious exuberance. He was trying to push a wad of Mexican bills into his hand, but Calvin kept pushing them back at him.

"I will take nothing," Calvin said. "All I ask is that you not speak of this day— to anyone. Your nephew has been returned to sanity, that is all anyone needs to know."

Joe and Maria reluctantly agreed, and Calvin said goodbye to Juan before he left. Juan would not meet his eyes, but stared only at the black bag he carried in his hand.

Calvin flew back to the United States with the bag in the carry-on compartment over his head. He worried that Joe and Maria might not keep their promise of secrecy. He had no way of knowing that Joe died of a heart attack that night or that Maria subsequently fell silent, never to speak a word again.

****

Father Carnahan did not like giving Mass. He imagined that, as a man who had served the church for a great many years, he should be spared the work and inconvenience of preparing a message or standing before a congregation every week. He preferred working with the children's choir and mentoring other youth within the church— activities that provided him access to what his darker habits required.

Through his reluctance, he had come to a sort of compromise with the parish: he would deliver only the Wednesday evening Mass and, in return, would be left alone on the weekends. The Wednesday Mass was sparsely attended at his church, a smattering of devout old retirees being the only ones to show up with any regularity. Half of them fell asleep during the service, and the other half were nearly senile. Carnahan had found that he could continually rotate the same three or four messages, and no one seemed to notice or care.

He arrived in the sanctuary unshaven and half-drunk, looked out upon his meager flock with blood-shot eyes, and began with the recitations that he could have done in his sleep, and sometimes did. There were fewer than twenty people in the pews that evening, the median age appearing to be about seventy-five. They bowed and crossed themselves and said "Amen" when they were supposed to, and Carnahan plowed forward with the ceremony with thoughts of getting done early.

He heard the sound of doors closing in the vestibule, imagined that someone was coming in late, but no one entered the sanctuary.

Calvin locked the doors to the outside. Then, for good measure, he wrapped a length of chain through the door handles and secured it with a padlock. Moving through the corridors of the church, he made sure that all of the other exterior doors were locked, blocking some of them with chairs and end tables. He knew he had time; even if Carnahan cut it short, he had plenty of time.

He returned to the suitcase that he had left in the vestibule. He opened it and took another inventory of the containers inside, each packed carefully in its own place. From among the vessels, he withdrew a thick piece of white chalk. With the chalk in hand, Calvin approached the high, oak doors to the sanctuary. Standing on his tiptoes, then kneeling low to the ground, he drew a circle that covered most of the surface of the double doors. Then, he carefully drew a five-pointed star within the circle, completing the pentagram.

Crouching, he drew a corresponding pentagram on the tile floor outside of the doors. He checked his watch, pulled a lighter from his pocket and lit five small candles that he took from the suitcase. Calvin placed a candle at the tip of each point on the pentagram.

Finally, he began to remove the containers from the case, placing each one within the star, every vessel in its chosen place. He ended by producing the five key artifacts: a pencil box, a coffee can, a tarnished cigarette case, a stoppered bottle, and the metronome. These he placed next to each of the burning candles.

The air in the vestibule hummed with power and energy. The candles flickered and danced about as if in a breeze, but the doors and windows were all closed and secured. Calvin checked his watch one more time, and then, he began to speak in low tones, incanting the names of the entities he had spent a lifetime collecting. He spoke with authority but also with an ingrained tenderness, like a parent instructing their children, and in fact, that is somewhat how he had come to think of himself.

His hands moved in the air above the containers, feeling the energy that was feverishly yearning to be set loose into the world once more. Even Agrogaut, his first, was there, still bound and waiting impatiently in the old cigar box. Calvin wondered at the symbols that he had crudely written on the box, the names of God. How was it possible that he did not have to believe? That the belief of the demons was enough to command and enslave them? How had he come to lead such an army?

He shook his head. It was no time for introspection or self-doubt. He had come so far, and now, the moment of reckoning had arrived. Calvin began to open the containers, starting at the center of the circle and working outwards. With each lid he opened or cork that he removed, a palpable sense of menace filled the air. There were hissings and cracklings and growls that he could not decide if they were in his head or if they were real.

Finally, he opened the containers at the points of the pentagram, ending with the metronome. When he removed the triangular cover from the device, the air went cold enough to freeze meat, the other demons fell silent, and the pendulum on the metronome began to rock, ticking back and forth, keeping time, setting pace, marking the beginning of the end.

Father Carnahan paused to yawn in the middle of his message. Perhaps it was brought on by the yawning of one of his parishioners, but he doubted he felt kindred enough to any of them for them to illicit such a response. He was simply tired and bored. The sanctuary had grown cold, and he made a mental note to berate the custodian in the morning for turning the thermostat too low.

In spite of the cold, someone in the pews had fallen asleep. Carnahan could hear their snoring from somewhere near the back. It did not bother him; it only made him glad that he got the Wednesday night Mass, where people could sleep comfortably and no one was likely to want to speak to him afterwards.

He trudged on through his notes, mentioning for the hundredth time the devoutness of John the Baptist. The snoring grew louder, echoing off the high walls and the vaulted ceiling. It was loud enough that it was causing others to whisper amongst themselves, and he could hear people shifting in their seats to find the cause of the sound.

Carnahan sighed with irritation and raised his eyes from his unnecessary notes. He could follow the stares of the congregants to the source of the noise and was surprised to see that the perpetrator was not asleep. In fact, the old woman making the terrible, wheezing, sawing sounds had her eyes wide open and her teeth bared. Her face was the picture of malevolence, trembling and twitching, wild. In that moment, it occurred to Father Carnahan that this withered octogenarian was not snoring. She was growling.

There were gasps and exclamations from others in the sanctuary. Someone cried out, "Claudine!" But before Carnahan could say anything of the matter, another congregant leapt to their feet and began screaming obscenities in a voice that seemed to come from a hundred throats. He was an old man, completely bald and pot-bellied. He wore a checkered tie, and as he let loose with such an awful and terrifying stream of invectives, he pulled up on the tie with one trembling hand. He seemed to be exerting all of his physical strength into pulling on the tie, as though he aimed to lift himself bodily from the floor. His face turned an alarming shade of red, and the man's wife began to strike at him, begging for him to stop.

Suddenly, the wife stopped her pleading as a new and different look came over her face. She underwent a full and total transformation: her posture changed, her head rolled back, and she began to laugh with such sincere and awful force that the sound overpowered her husband's curses and the growling and snarling of the old woman in back.

Carnahan was utterly confused and frightened in no small measure. He lifted his arms above his head and called out to the room, "Everyone, everyone please be calm. What is going on here? What is the matter with you?"

But the congregants were not listening to him. They were getting up from their seats and gathering their coats and hats, tucking their Bibles away into the pew backs. Or they were rushing over to their suddenly afflicted friends, calling out their names, desperate to help.

And then, they were not.

One by one, and with rapid intensity, each aged and frail member of that Wednesday evening flock was transformed, overtaken, possessed with a vigor and wrath unlike anything that Father Carnahan had ever imagined. They turned upon one another, screaming and cackling, tearing at faces and bodies with old and gnarled hands. One old crone vomited in the center aisle, a continuous projectile stream that seemed like it would never end.

As two elderly men came crashing together in front of the altar, one biting at the other's fingers, the second alternately laughing and speaking in indecipherable Latin, Father Carnahan ducked down behind the lectern. He sank to the floor on his creaky, old knees and clutched at his chest. His breathing was coming hard, and his heart pounded. What was happening? The sounds from the nave were horrid, otherworldly, and increasing in intensity and volume.

He saw a route, a chance for escape, and he crawled behind the skirts of the altar just as a withered hand reached out to grasp at his robes, the fingernails wet with blood. Carnahan shed his stole, losing it to the clutching hand, and slithered down the three short steps that led to the altar. Crawling like a soldier on his elbows, legs splayed and pumping behind him, he ducked beneath the pews and struggled toward the back of the room, avoiding anywhere that he saw the feet of his deranged flock, stomping or dancing or trembling in awful paroxysms of evil.

Father Carnahan lowered his head and strove onward, his eyes only on the doors at the back of the sanctuary, his thoughts only on escape. He did not understand what was going on, nor did he need to. The only thing he knew was that he needed to get out of the church before any of the parishioners could get hold of him. He needed time to confess. He needed more time before his demise could be embraced. Life was supposed to be much longer — at least that was what he had always believed.

Calvin could not resist. He had cracked open the doors to the sanctuary and peeked in as his collected entities invisibly pounced upon the unsuspecting souls within. They had been pent up for so long, had been deprived of chaos and destruction. They fed so quickly and easily upon the fear and superstition in the sanctuary that Calvin was thrilled at the look on Father Carnahan's face as his congregation disintegrated into hellish debauchery and madness before his very eyes.

The metronome continued to tick back and forth behind him as Calvin stood in awe of the terrible scene unfolding in the church. The sanctuary was cold, but the vestibule was far colder, and a wind seemed to rush past Calvin, chilling his spine and ruffling his hair.

He saw Carnahan slink down from the altar like a snake. He watched as the old priest army crawled under the rows and rows of pews, even as his flock clawed and thrashed and fell in blood and terror. It seemed that a thousand voices were erupting from that cavernous room, where no more than two-dozen people had entered. All of the rage and pain of hell had filled that sanctimonious space and now was flushing out the agent of sin that Calvin most despised.

Calvin had not laid eyes on Father Vincent Carnahan in many, many years. He had done his best not to think of him, even to the point of convincing himself that he had forgotten the man who abused and shamed him, who broke him when he was just a young boy with two strikes against him, a kid that needed a chance in the world.

But now, as he watched Carnahan emerge head first from beneath the last row of pews, he remembered his mission; he felt the weight of decades of denial and shame. Calvin had gone through the motions as though he were in a dream. He collected and told himself he did not know why. He plotted and pretended he did not know the ends to his means. Now, the ends looked up at him with fearful and bloodshot eyes.

He swung the door wide open, and the metronome stopped ticking.

There was a moment of stillness in the church. A pause, while all of the possessed congregants fell still, their inhabited bodies turning to bear witness to what was about to happen in the back of the sanctuary.

The silence was deafening, coming abruptly on the heels of such chaos and rage, but there was nothing peaceful about the quiet. It was charged with animosity and an unspeakable hatred. The old and possessed slowly gathered toward the rear, forming a rough semicircle around the back doors, where two men stared at one another. One was old, and the other was much older. The older man laid prone on the floor, and they recognized him as the priest who had been drumming on when they came in. The younger man was their keeper, their captor and their enemy, though he seemed not to realize the last part.

The time had finally come. Their savior was loosed and ready to begin.

A hard and icy wind began to swirl around the massive room, picking up speed and violence; picking up hymnals and tracts; picking up vestments and chalices. A veritable cyclone of symbolic detritus whipped about in the air, and the younger man showed fear in his eyes, incomprehension. The older man's gaze had begun to lose its determination, as he was seeing through the veil and seemed to have glimpsed the doom that was to come.

The doors exploded from their hinges, and the Behemoth entered the room as both illusion and flesh. It flickered between visible and invisible, took on form and shape and also melted or evaporated from sight like a wraith or a nightmare. It had gray flesh or no flesh, its bones could be seen, as well as its long and tarnished teeth. But, at the same time, it was not there, had never been there, but the sheer terror would remain in this space forever. This was now the place of the Behemoth. It was not a church, could never be a place of worship again, for the End was beginning.

There opened a hole in the floor, but really, it was a hole in space and time. It opened between the two men, and now, the wind and the litter and debris rushed down into the hole, pulling everything, even light and hope and faith. Down. Down. Forever down.

The Behemoth roared, the lights went out, and the stained-glass windows burst out of their frames and filled the churchyard with razor sharp and colorful snow. It crouched above the two men who perhaps could see it but were too transfixed on the hole in the earth and the terror that lay beyond, so they were not at all prepared when he swatted them into the void forever, and no one would ever know if Father Calvin Berkeley and the man who had ruined him, the one he hated with such a bottomless passion, ended up in the same hell.

THE CAMP

Hank's first stroll through the wreckage told him everything he needed to know. The world wasn't the same anymore. It had been shredded, ripped, exploded, and devoured into an unrecognizable mess. Not exactly the sight he wanted to wake up to after an eleven-day nap.

The first shock was the Rialto, a local movie theater that had somehow survived decades and decades of competition from gigantic chains, video rentals, then DVDs, and, finally, streaming, only to succumb to a single blast.

And here it was, shattered into a million shards of multicolored glass and splintered wooded panels. Next to that was the liquor store—now just a collapsed building flooded by various sticky liquids and a fast-food restaurant, its smashed golden arches the only evidence that it was ever more than a pile of smoking rubble.

Hank shook his head as he walked past the bodies lying strewn around in all directions, wondering if anybody else had survived. After an hour of walking, the answer seemed to be "no." He heard nothing, saw no movement—human or animal. He spotted the occasional carcass and a few corpses, but it seemed nobody made it out alive.

Before planning for the collapse, Hank wondered what it might have been like to be the only survivor. It would be lonely, to be sure. But even without others to share the world with him, it was better to be alive and alone than dead with the others. Right?

The longer Hank walked, the less sure he was about the answer.

He stared long and hard at the now-mangled and charred Ridgely Park, its green hills plowed into an uneven mound of dirt, dying grass and hands jutting out reaching for God knows what.

Hank thought about all the time he'd spent there, games of tag, walks with George, his Doberman. His gaze locked so heavy on the destroyed landscape that footfalls coming from down the street nearly sent him crashing to the ground in shock.

He straightened and found shelter behind a rubble of rusted steel, then slowly eased his head forward, giving himself a view of what was happening down the street.

There was a group of them, too far away to discern details, but they looked like a group of hoodlums, clad in tatters, bodies swaying with menace as they laughed like jackals and howled their machismo at high volume.

It seemed they had a captive—although, again, he could not be sure from this distance. But he could spot reluctance and apprehension emanating from a smaller body being dragged along behind the group.

Their words were also difficult to make sense of. Probably just empty boasts, anyway.

In any case, Hank didn't have time to figure things out. The group or "gang," or whatever they were, was now strutting in his direction. And remaining hidden behind the slender pile he found himself behind wouldn't be an option for long. He had to get away, get back to his bunker.

The bunker was a safe place. He'd built it with the intention of shielding himself against the roughest of external threats—natural or otherwise. If it could stand eleven days of the earth being ravaged by an unprecedented torment, it could survive a group of street thugs. It contained walls of re-enforced steel, along with buttresses that simply couldn't be kicked, blown, or beaten down.

But none of that mattered if he couldn't get there.

The group was closer now, and he had to get across the street to reach the bunker. From there, he'd have a chance. Getting shot in the back was a possibility but only if he waited too long, gave them too much time to advance.

Hank bolted across the street, head tucked low, hands over his head.

The plan—if you could call it that—was simply to run and keep running until he reached the bunker. But that wasn't so easy to carry out.

A snag jutting from the sidewalk clanked against his ankle, sending him tumbling into the glass-littered concrete.

Luckily, a sideways, mangled dumpster was close enough to crawl behind before attracting any attention. Once there, he picked his head up to see the gang in stunned silence.

They pointed vengeful fingers into every direction at once, as if determined to find this fleet-footed stranger but unable to do so.

As he had before, he slowly edged his head from behind the hunk of steel in hopes of giving himself a wider view.

But it only gave his hiding place away.

His bunker was hidden and sheltered behind the door of what used to be a grocery store—right under the floor, which meant all he had to do was get inside the building.

But first, he had to get across the street.

Somebody shouted, "get him!" and he heard a flurry of footsteps locked in rhythmic precision. He ran toward the street, legs moving in fast-motion, gunshots clapping behind him. The building was now closer than ever, thirty feet away.

He kept scurrying, breathless, strained. Ten feet away, now five...

He clawed with the key, unable to bring his clumsy hands

into synched-up movements. More shots, more footsteps, he was stabbing the key now, shoving it, angry. Now, the key was in, but he'd have to shove it open, harder, then harder still.

After a final bang, the door swung open, and the momentum of his shoves sent him to the building's floor face first.

He slammed the door shut, then locked it. Without the energy needed to stay on his feet, he crawled toward the bunker's opening, hearing glass shatter all around him.

Once the thugs smashed nearly all the glass away, their shouts were amplified into animalistic howls.

He reached the bunker's opening next to what was once isle seventeen. After quickly tapping in the numeric code, the steel door swung open, and he dove inside, taking a graceless tumble down the ladder.

He hit the bunker's floor and waited for the automatic door to close. It took five seconds—just as it had been programmed.

The stainless-steel door sealed off the noise and the danger above. He was safe.

He'd never been more exhausted in his life. But he was alive. And, maybe, that's what made him cry.

****

Hank had a feeling sleep that night would not be easy.

This was, after all, the first time he'd seen the horrific aftermath the world had become. The images of wreckage, devastation, and heartbreaking human loss were unlike anything he'd ever seen. He laid in bed, eyes wide and studying the patterns on the ceiling, pretending he hadn't witnesses what he'd witnessed.

But it got worse.

He also began recalling the names and faces of those left behind. His girlfriend, Sharon, who thought his bunker idea, and by extension him, was crazy.

They'd argue late into the night about whether or not there was reason to believe the world was coming to an end. He tried to convince her with images on the news, information from trusted sources, everything. But in the end, he just gave up. He couldn't convince her the danger of a coming collapse was real. In the midst of their most heated arguments—most of which, she won—he struggled to convince himself of this possibility. He'd wondered if she was right, wondered if the fear he'd stored up had any basis in reality at all.

The same happened with his mother and two older brothers. They also thought he'd lost his mind. Just like his friends, neighbors, co-workers at the office, and, when he quit the office to devote more time to constructing his bunker, his new co-workers at the factory held the same opinion. Hank wasn't somebody to take seriously. He'd never before had more regret over being right. Because it meant being alone.

He'd heard about others making bunkers, but his stroll through town suggested none of them had done it the right way. Most bunkers weren't strong and solid enough. They weren't preparing for a hurricane or a riot. They were preparing to survive the end of time. And most bunkers weren't designed for that. Hank's was.

Then, there was the girl.

As he lay there in bed, the sound of her desperate calls for help echoed in his head.

In the blur of frantic action, he hadn't noticed her voice. But now with time to remember it all, it was right there. Loud, shrill, sad, nearly defeated.

At times, it wasn't clear if the sound in his head was the girl's actual voice outside the bunker or just memories reverberating in his head. But either way, there was no chance of him getting any sleep that night.

Hank got up and did a quick inventory of things in his bunker. He checked the food supply, the generator-operated heating unit. He checked the lights, making sure that the generator would give him as much light as needed, and he also checked the candles to ensure that he would be prepared in case the generator let him down.

He resisted the urge of a midnight snack, knowing that his food supply was designed to last approximately sixty years. It seemed unlikely that he'd be around longer than that, but with enough midnight snacks, the number could be chipped away.

In the end, he succumbed to the urge to open up a bag of popcorn. He sat there, remembering how much fun it was to stay up past his bedtime with his big brother, Eddie. They'd eat popcorn and talk about things Hank was sure older kids talked about all the time. Cars, girls, PG-13 movies, and football.

After a few more fruitless hours of lying in bed, Hank laid there, licking the popcorn's salt from his fingertips and wondering how differently things may have turned out if he'd been persistent with Sharon. Or Eddie. Or his mother.

What if he'd had the courage to stay on them, to persuade them to follow his path? It was too late to find out the answer to that question.

But it wasn't too late for the girl.

He snapped out of bed and starting pacing, wondering what

was happening to her right now. Could he find them? Could he save the girl?

Within minutes, he had scrambled into clothes and climbed out of his bunker, strapped with a revolver at his hip.

Taking a gaze at the mess made by the gang of thugs, he could hear them without even leaving the building. They screamed drunken streams into the night, singing, laughing, daring anyone to come near. It wouldn't be hard to find them, and—assuming she was still alive—it wouldn't be hard to find the girl.

The building's glass door had been smashed into nothing but a still frame. The windows were also almost completely gone. If he angled his body just right, he could crouch and seek out the source of the noise.

They were about a block and a half down the street, taking turns kicking at an old refrigerator. There were about eight of them, scruffy-looking, young, dressed in rags. The girl was there, too, crouched in a ball, her face in her hands, crying.

Hank sat there and watched for a while, putting together a plan. It would have to be a good one because he had only six bullets in the chamber. It didn't occur to him to pack extra.

Even if he'd been a good shot, hitting more than one would be tough—especially with them being armed. He counted two guns. One guy with a holstered pistol, another with a rifle tucked under his arm while he sat on the ground and chugged whiskey.

After a quick scan of the environment, the wheels started shifting in Hank's brain. He saw a segment of a brick wall off to the side that could offer shelter from a barrage of bullets. He also saw that the girl was not under anybody's control, meaning she could slip free as soon as the gunfire began.

Hank took a deep breath, then counted to three with the

intention of snapping the plan into action as soon as he was done.

But he froze at three, unable to act.

So, he counted again and, this time, didn't let anyone down. He raced to the segment of the brick wall, and before anyone could react, he crouched there and started firing.

He sent one thug to the ground and quickly tagged a second in his shoulder before anyone could figure out where the shots were coming from.

As bedlam unfolded, the next shot sailed over everyone's head. The girl sprang free, and others reached for their guns.

The fourth shot hit somebody's ankle and sent him to the ground as the others scrambled away.

Only two shots left now. But there was also good news: his targets hadn't found his hiding place. Their eyes darted around, unsure who was attacking them and from where.

Hank stopped shooting, decided to preserve his bullets and get out when he could. He could see the girl five feet away from him as she cowered behind a hunk of steel. He waved her toward him, but she just stayed there, shivering. "Come on!" he whispered loudly, waving a second time.

Shellshocked by the gunshots, she wasn't going to move. He'd have to go after her—even if it meant risking becoming a target himself.

He tried to calm himself with a deep breath, then fired a shot before racing out from behind his shield. He held a hand out for her, but she still wouldn't come. "Would you come on! You want to get out of here, don't you?"

Still no reaction, so he grabbed her by the blouse and yanked her away. A few shots followed him, one skipped between his legs and the second tagged the heel of boot, kicking his leg from under him and bringing him into a face first tumble.

No choice but to fire his last shot. He turned and pulled the trigger as he fought to get back to his feet. A loud, hard grunt suggested he'd hit somebody as he scampered away, still yanking the girl with him.

As they reached the grocery building, he could hear the thugs approaching, but they were too far away to do any damage. It didn't help that the girl was now screaming, giving their location away.

He clamped her mouth shut with a hand and shoved her inside with him. But the struggle wasn't yet over. She needed to be pushed and pulled and tugged all the way to and then down the bunker's opening.

Once she reached the bottom of the bunker's ladder, she scrambled away in the dark, bolting away from his grip. Hank flipped on the lights and gave chase.

But it wouldn't be easy to find her. He checked every closet, every pantry, every possible nook and cranny and didn't find her. Until he got to the bathroom.

Once in there, she'd taken down the still curtain rod and wielded it like a Louisville slugger. She scowled at him, eyes narrowed, teeth bared. "Back up!" she growled. "Or I'll knock you out, I swear!"

"Would you give me that!"

She took a swing, missing Hank's face by about a half an inch.

"I told you, back up or you get it in the face!"

"I don't understand this!" Hank yelled. "I just rescued you. And this is the thanks I get!"

"Rescued me for what?" she asked, her face trembling in anticipation of his answer. "Why did you bring me back here?"

"Because I didn't want those guys hurting you!"

The trembling on her face accelerated. "I don't buy that! Why are you holding me here? What do you want from me?"

Puzzled, Hank had no answer for her. He just backed away slowly, hands up.

"What do you want from me?" Soon, the girl was nearly screaming herself hoarse. "Tell me! What do you want from me?"

Hanks lowered his voice and softened his tone. "I don't want to hurt you. I swear. Look, I'm just like you. I survived whatever it was you survived, and here we both are. That's all. Just give me that rod and let me help you. Please."

The girl collapsed into tears on the bathroom floor, letting the shower rod fall from her grip and hit the hardwood floor with a loudly echoing *clank!*

He tried to hug her, and she pulled away at first, only allowing her hands to be touched by him. The tears kept flowing and flowing. Her head landed on his shoulder and muffled sobs went on for nearly an hour. Hank could tell there was a story she needed to tell him. But she wasn't ready to share it. For now, there were only more tears.

****

After all of the chaos that had taken place, Hank needed sleep to compensate for the sleep he had missed hours earlier. The girl stayed in his bunker but refused on sleep on the sofa—or anywhere else. Instead, she stayed crouched in the corner, eyes wide and body ready to react to defend itself against anything.

Her face, although more relaxed than it had been, was still in an eternal state of alertness. Her reddish-brown hair circled her face in untamed curls, and her clothes were covered in dirt and grime, giving her an even more feral appearance. But she was far from intimidating—her small, skinny frame prevented that from being a possibility.

Before going to sleep, Hank told her, "Look, I get that you're not cool with going to sleep, and well, obviously, you don't have to, but I need sleep."

She nodded.

"Just do me a favor and try not to have any surprises for me when I wake up. Can you handle that?"

She nodded again.

"Great," he said. "Good night."

Another nod.

"I suppose a goodnight kiss is out of the question?" he asked.

The girl's body tensed into a defensive ball.

"I'm kidding. I'll see you in the morning. Or whatever it is when I wake up."

She nodded slightly.

"By the way, what is your name?" he asked.

"Wendy," she answered, her voice just above a whisper.

"Okay. Goodnight, Wendy. You can call me Hank."

She nodded again, her face as cold and sharp as it was when she first entered the bunker. He half-smiled to himself, wondering what it would be like to spend his life with somebody afraid to speak to him. But he was already asleep before seriously considering it.

****

Hank woke up to find his guest curled asleep in the hallway leading to the kitchen. He crouched to eye-level and studied her face, wondering if her story could be seen.

But no. She was as opaque asleep as she had been awake. It was as if she wore her protective shell to bed with her like a pair of pajamas.

He rose, preparing to step into the kitchen when Wendy's body jerked itself awake. "Huh?" she grunted, hands defensively lifted, eyes wide.

"It's okay," he said, voice soft. "It's just me. Nobody's going to hurt you."

Wendy took a glance around the hallway and climbed to her feet. "Can I… um, clean up?" she asked.

"Sure." he pointed down the hallway. "I was going to make some breakfast. I was thinking maybe waffles or pancakes, but I've got plenty of eggs saved up, so I think I'll cook up some—"

The bathroom door slammed shut behind her quick escape.

"So… eggs, it is."

"I have to say," he shouted to the bathroom. "When I first put up this bunker, I thought I'd possibly go out of my mind without anybody here to talk to."

No answer from the bathroom, but Hank knew his guest

heard him. Although with the shower water now coming on, he'd have to speak louder.

"And it's funny, you know," he continued, scrambling the eggs and preparing condensed milk in two cups. "I was never really a talkative guy. Some people would even say I was shy —especially around girls. But there's something about spending time alone that makes a fella miss conversation. Even with somebody that's not really talking back that much."

More silence from the bathroom.

"Or somebody that's not really talking back at all."

Once he finished the scrambling the eggs and portioning out the condensed milk, he set the table, then took a seat and waited for his guest to emerge from the bathroom.

It took about ten minutes, but Wendy came out, her face decorated with a tight grin. She was wearing the same clothes as before, and her soaking wet hair was tucked in a knot.

"I've got an extra pair of pajamas if you want any," he said. "They may be a little too big for you, but—"

"No, that's fine. You've really done enough already. Thank you." Wendy took a seat at the table and sheepishly started to eat, her eyes darting around like a kitten sneaking a nibble from the family dinner.

"Probably not the best scrambled eggs you've ever had. Not that scrambled eggs are even that great when they're at their best. But you know how it is. When you load up on food, the key is how long something will last, not how good it tastes."

Wendy smiled. "These are fine. Thank you." But the smile faded quickly, and she put her food back on the plate, sending her gaze somewhere else. "I'm sorry I'm not much company. I just can't stop thinking about… all the people."

Hank leaned in to her, spoke gently. "You mean those guys? The gang? I'm sure they must have been some really—"

She shook her head. "Not them," she said. "I mean, not just them." She took a deep breath and made eye contact with Hank for the first time. "There's a whole bunch of people. They survived—just like I did. But they..."

Afraid he'd spook her, Hank said nothing, keeping silent as her words came out organically and unhurriedly.

"They... were all together. In this big dome. Thousands of us. This was about fifty, maybe seventy-five miles away from here. We were all there. It was like a little city. Everybody helping each other out, giving food and medical help to anybody in need."

"But something happened to them?"

Wendy nodded. "These guys came in and took over, just took control of everybody. Put everybody to work—even the old people and kids. It was like a big... slave camp or something. People tried to escape—and a few people did. Like those guys you saw."

"You mean those thugs? The guys who were holding you captive?"

"Yeah. I escaped with them. It was about thirty of us, a few women, a few kids. We came up with this big plan of how we'd wait till they were distracted and then run off, then we'd be free. And we were. Kind of. I mean, some of us were freer than others."

Hank's eyes softened. "I guess that explains why you were leery of me when I helped you get free from the guys."

Wendy nodded, her eyes on the scrambled eggs below.

"Is that slave camp—or whatever it is—still there?"

"I have no idea. But it makes me sad to think about all

those people." She got up from the table. "I don't think I can eat anymore. But thank you for the breakfast." Wendy turned away from the table, burying her face in her hands and sobbing.

Hank couldn't eat anymore either. "Look, Wendy, if it makes you feel any better, I've lost lots of people, too."

She lifted her angry eyes to his. "These people aren't lost! They're still alive."

"Yes, but there's nothing we can do about that."

"Isn't there? You helped me. Can you help these people?"

"The way you made it sound, there's a whole army holding these people captive," he said. "What do you want me to do?"

"It's not an army. It's just a handful of people…"

"Yes, but if they have control over everybody, it might as well be an army."

She nodded her head and swallowed tears. "I suppose you're right."

A deadly silence fell between them.

Hank asked, "Is there any of your family back there? Kids? Husband? Anything like that?"

"A few friends, yeah. But I lost my family right away. None of them survived. Husband died when he went to go pick up our daughter from nursery school. Both of them blew up in this big blast. Parents, two brothers, cousins, all gone."

They shared eye contact that seemed to warm them both. They clasped hands. "How many people do you suppose are still back there?"

Wendy shrugged her shoulders. "A couple thousand maybe."

Hank lost himself in deep thought, planning things out. He figured with the element of surprise, they could possibly take the gang over, free some of the people, perhaps all of them.

Or maybe not.

There was also a possibility they could get killed in the process—or taken captive themselves. But what was the alternative? Cowering in fear, afraid to leave the bunker? That was no way to live, certainly no way Hank wanted to live, especially knowing he had a chance to save people.

Another thing to consider was the gang of thugs who resided right down the street. He asked Wendy, "What can you tell me about those guys who were holding you?"

"Nothing really," she said. "They're just a random bunch of guys who broke out of the camp."

"How did they do it?"

"They managed to get into the weapons of the group that was holding everybody. They stole a bunch of explosives and guns and whatnot."

"What did they do with all that stuff?"

"They stashed it away in the building they stay in."

More ideas swirled in Hank's head. He wondered if there was a way they could sneak into the building, steal some—or maybe all—of the ammunition. "You think you could lead me to the building, help me sneak in after they've gone to sleep?"

Wendy's face twisted as if stumped by a tricky math problem.

"Look, I understand I'm asking a lot of you—especially after all you've been through, but I'm going to need you to be brave. I can't do this alone."

Her face hardened into concrete. This wasn't the same frightened girl of only a few hours ago. "Whatever you need, I'm with you."

"Perfect. We'll wait till later tonight, after they've gone to sleep."

****

Hank and Wendy crept out of the bunker somewhere around 2 AM. She pointed to the building where the guys slept, and they eased a little closer, Hank's antennae tuned to any sounds or sights that stood out.

He saw nothing and heard nothing. A glance behind the hollowed-out windows of the convenience store that they all slept in revealed six bodies on the floor, all seemingly asleep. A few of them may have been awake, but it would have likely been difficult for them to jump to their feet and cause a problem.

Roughly fifty feet away from their building, Wendy leaned into him and whispered, "They keep all the weapons and stuff in the room down the hallway."

Hank nodded, plans taking shape in his head.

After about a minute of looking at the building, figuring out the arrangements of the bodies inside, he had a concrete blueprint for how things would go. He'd slip into a side door, step into the room with the ammunition, and take what was needed —figuring that wouldn't be much more than a rifle or two, maybe some spare bullets or grenades.

In the event that a few guys woke up, he'd improvise, and since he was in a room full of ammunition, the improvisation would be easy. All he'd have to do was keep his ears open, make sure nobody moved without him knowing about it. No matter how bad the situation, he'd have the element of surprise.

He leaned closer to Wendy and whispered, "Here's what I need from you: I need you to keep your eyes open, watching the guys sleeping in the front room. I'll check back from time to time to make sure everything is okay. Give me the OK sign to let me know everything is fine."

"What if it isn't fine?"

"You turn back and run like hell to the bunker. Don't worry about me. If I don't see the sign, I'll assume there's a problem, and I'll adjust accordingly."

After thinking for a second, Wendy offered a weak nod.

"You sure you're fine with this?" he asked.

"Well... not really, but I don't suppose we have a choice, do we? We're going to have to do this whether we're fine or not."

Hank smirked a little, then took a deep breath preparing for the journey inside.

Wendy dropped behind a pile of steel rubble, and Hank, head crouched low, crept across the street. He ducked to the building's side door and pressed his body against the wall, giving Wendy a look.

After getting the sign, he slipped through the side door, not a difficult task with the glass shattered away. The biggest challenge was stepping across the shards along the floor without making too much noise.

He moved in tiny half steps as quietly as he could, then reached the room full of ammunition Wendy told him about. The image of all those rifles, machine guns, bazookas, and grenades nearly took his breath away.

Figuring there was no time to be picky, he swiftly grabbed an automatic machine gun laid against the rear wall, a belt of bullets laying at its side. But just as he began to strap it over his shoulder, a high-pitched wail came from outside. "Haaaaank!"

That was Wendy, no doubt about it.

He glanced out of the window to see a silhouetted pair of arms behind a pile of rubble waving frantically.

Then came a second voice—this one deeper, calmer, more filled with menace—behind him. "Don't move, cowboy,"

Hank instinctively lifted his arms, slowly turning his head to find the source of the voice.

It was one of the thugs, a rifle aimed at Hank's eyes. The man gave a low chuckle but not at Hank. Something outside seemed to amuse him.

Wendy had dropped to the street, a streak of blood pooling from her mouth. Another armed goon held a rifle on her, also chuckling.

"Looks like you stumbled into the wrong place, buddy."

Hank felt the butt of a rifle slam against his temple, sending him straight to the floor before he could find anything resembling balance. He laid there as the world wavered in and out.

He heard a conversation happening just above him.

One guy said, "Should we just kill them?"

"Wait till morning."

"Morning?"

"Yeah, it's too late to be dragging bodies out to the…"

And then, he was out.

****

After a chaotic shuffle of bodies, Wendy and Hank were held captive in the room of ammunition by a guy with the machine gun Hank previously had strapped to his shoulder.

The guy boasted a scruffy beard that nearly reached midway down his chest, and the rest of his face was pockmarked, scarred, and tattooed.

His lifeless eyes swept back and forth from Wendy to Hank, his two seated captives, as he kept the machine gun at hip level. He didn't seem happy to be stuck with this job while the others went back to sleep in the front room.

"I'm really sorry," Wendy said, her voice shaky, maybe on the verge of tears.

"Sorry for what?" Hank answered.

"I know you told you me to run back to the bunker if something happened, but I just couldn't… "

"It's okay."

"I just couldn't leave you alone like that."

"It's okay," Hank said. "That bruise on your mouth looked pretty brutal. You doing okay?"

"Not really. But we're alive, right?"

"You guys have a bunker?" the guard grunted, catching his hostages off-guard.

"Uh… yeah," Hanks said. "Why?"

"My brother had a bunker," he said, a tinge of sadness in his voice.

"Did he… make it?"

"Yeah. But no, not really."

"What does that mean?"

"It means he lived, but he didn't make it out of that… place."

"You mean that camp?" Hank asked. "The place they were holding everybody?"

The guy's breathing grew heavy. He was holding back sobs, so it seemed a good time to stop asking questions.

Minutes of uneasy silence passed, and the guy's frozen face slowly melted. A tear trickled down his cheek before being smothered by his massive beard.

Hank glanced around at all the ammunition. The grenades, the rifles, the boxes of rounds. The endless supply of small explosives. He whistled as if admiring a beautiful woman's body. "Sure got lots of weaponry here."

The remark removed the sadness from his voice, along with a throat clearing, then the thug answered, "Yep. Just about all we'll ever need."

"Need for what?"

"What are you getting at?"

"I mean, is there a plan?"

"Yeah. We plan on not getting killed. Or captured by those bastards at the camp."

"You guys ever think about using these weapons on the offensive?"

"You mean attacking the guys at the camp?"

"Sure," Hank said. "There aren't that many of them from what I've heard."

"There's enough."

"So… nobody here has ever talked about it. Going back and rescuing those at the camp?"

"In case you ain't notice, buddy. The folks around here ain't the rescuing type. Half of us were locked up in prison, and the other half shoulda' been."

"Yeah, but you all had family there, right? Your brother, for example?"

A nerve had been struck. The guard's jaw tightened at the mention of his brother. "What about him?"

Hank paused before speaking again, knowing he was moving down a dangerous path. "If it were me, and I had family there — brother, parents, kids, wife, whatever—and I had all this ammunition, I'd be fighting to save them. Unless…"

The guard brought his angry face inches away from Hank's, his voice now a menacing growl. "Unless what?"

Screwing up all the courage he could find, Hank said, "Unless you're some kind of coward or something."

"He didn't mean that!" Wendy shrieked.

"Yes, I did," Hank said, matching the guard's menace. "The fact that you could sit here knowing all those people—even your own family—needs your help while you sit back and do nothing… well, the only word for that is 'coward.'"

"Boy, that's some words you really need to take back if you want to be around much longer."

"But you know it's true. Don't you?"

The guy said nothing. But Hank could see a flutter sneaking into his eyes. He spoke again, this time sounding softer, almost apologetic. "Since you seem to know so Goddamn much about some place you ain't never been, tell me what the hell you'd do."

Composing himself, Hank took a deep breath. "Well, for starters you could get a few ringers in the camp."

"Ringers?"

"Yeah, a few fake prisoners. That way, you could create some kind of distraction inside and attack from the outside at the same time."

"And you think that would work?"

"I guarantee it."

The guard's stone face erupted into a low chuckle. "You're nuts."

"No, I'm serious. You let me plan this thing, and I'll have your brother out—along with everybody else."

No more laughter from the guard. He rose to his feet. He kept his eyes on Wendy and Hank as if sizing them up. Then, he called down the hallway. "Jeffers!"

Roughly a minute later, a set of heavy footsteps came down the hallway. A disheveled, tall, slender man came through the doorway. He didn't seem happy to have been awaken. "What's the problem, Zeke?"

The guard, Zeke, pointed to Hank with his machine gun, then addressed him, "Tell him what you told me. About the camp."

"The camp?" Jeffers asked.

"That's what he called that place. That place we 'scaped from."

Jeffers stretched though a long yawn. "This better be good."

"Tell him," Zeke said.

"Well," Hank said, "I was just saying there's a way we could rescue some of the people there—maybe all of them if all goes well."

"Are you crazy?" Jeffers asked.

Hank repeated his words to Jeffers, selling his idea with bravado. Deep down, he knew his plan was a long shot, but his options were limited, and if nothing else, it would give him another shot at the idea originally hatched by Wendy. And most importantly, it was keeping the two of them alive.

Jeffers said nothing after hearing Hank's words. But his eyes narrowed in a way that suggested he was weighing things in consideration.

"What do you think?" Hank asked. "Personally, I think it can work if we just stick together. It's really important that we all act as a team here and not get too—"

"Shut up," Jeffers said. "We'll hash everything out in the morning. For now, just get some sleep. I don't want you dozing off in the middle of the whole thing."

Hank released a deep breath of relief. "Yes, I understand… I'll just… get to sleep now."

****

It seemed only a matter of minutes before morning came

and shook everybody awake with a blinding, cloudless sky. Zeke was right there with the machine gun, looking as though he hadn't blinked since Hank saw him last. "Morning, Zeke," Hank said.

Zeke nodded politely, and by now, the crowd had begun to gather around him, Zeke, and Wendy. Everybody was armed and sending menacing glares to Hank. Jeffers stepped in front of everybody and crouched to address him face to face. "The gang's all here, buddy. Now's the time to put everything into motion. What's the first move?"

"Breakfast would be nice," Hank said, listening to his stomach growl.

Without breaking eye contact, Jeffers said, "Jett, give the man one of those old burgers we found."

An answer came from the rear of the crowd. "But those were —"

"Just wipe the mold off of it and give the man his breakfast."

A sandwich was tossed Hank's way, landing on his chest then bouncing on the floor where it split into a messy collection of meat and half-green bread. "Actually," Hank said, "I've got some real food at my bunker."

"You got enough for everybody?" Jeffers asked.

Hank took a look around, did the math in his head, and understood the problems this would cause for his plans to remained stocked for multiple years. But it didn't seem he had any other answer to the question. "Sure."

"Alright," Jeffers said. "Breakfast at Hank's, then we go to war."

****

In Hank's bunker, Jeffers' guys ate as if it had been months since they'd had a decent meal, wolfing down bread, eggs, pancakes, oatmeal, and anything else they could get their hands on.

Hank sat back from the crowd, watching and wondering what was next. Wendy joined him, a look of worry reaching her face. "How confident are you in this plan?" she asked him, her voice hushed and shaky.

"Honestly, Wendy," he said, "I have no idea how things are going to go. I don't even know how these guys would react in an actual battle situation. Hell, I don't know how I'd react. I'd never shot anybody before in my life before — before that night when I came to get you."

A tiny smile wrinkled her mouth. "Well, you did pretty good that night if I recall."

"Thanks."

"My daddy used to say, 'you never know what you're gonna' do with a gun till it gets in your hands and you have to do something.'"

He turned to her, watched her eyes warm a little at the mention of her father. "You ever get one in your hands and have to do something?"

She replied with a cocky nod. "Sure did. My daddy taught me well."

Hank had to see for himself, so the two of them snuck away from the gang's breakfast and went back and forth with a rifle, taking shots at beer bottles lined up on a distant fence.

Hank hit two of the ten lined up. Wendy hit the remaining seven.

A group of footsteps crept up behind them. Hank turned to find the gang watching her shoot.

"Guys," he said, "We've got our lead sharpshooter."

An eruption of laughter followed. "Come on, dude," Jeffers said. "You've got a skirt on sniper duty?"

"Anybody want to challenge her for the job?"

One by one, they each tried and failed.

"Like I said, guys," Hank repeated, "We've got our lead sharpshooter. The rest of you, follow her lead. She always takes the first shot."

Sour faces all around.

"You're going to surround the camp and wait for any kind of commotion you hear or see," Hank said. "I'll do what I can to keep the guys in plain view and on the outside. You're going to pick these guys off any chance you get."

Jeffers stepped forward and addressed Hank. "Okay, enough talk. It's time to make this happen. You're going to get into that camp and do what you need to do. We'll be waiting on the outside to react to anything that happens. And if you don't make it out, I don't know what to tell you. You just don't."

Hank nodded, doing his best to keep his face stoic and without visible panic.

Jeffers nodded his head forward. "The camp's that way. Should be about a walk of thirty minutes. Soon as you get close, we'll slip back and find a place to hide."

The gang marched together in near silence. The walk's actual duration felt closer to an hour.

When they reached the camp, there was doubt they'd gotten there. The land ahead was mostly flattened and cleared away except for a small dome in the distance. Without a word, the guys all found shelter in the bushes with Wendy leading the way.

Before he stepped on, Hank turned. "Am I going in alone?"

Jeffers said, "Of course you are. We need as many armed guys out here as we can get."

"Maybe not," Hank said. "Two people inside might be better. We can team up and—"

Jeffers brought his angry face to Hank's. "What the hell's going on, man? You getting cold feet? I thought you were so confident this plan was perfect."

"I am," Hank said, trying to mask the crack in his voice. "I just wanted to know if I was going in alone. That's all."

Zeke stepped forward. "Naw, man," he said. "You're not going in alone."

"Zeke, we need you back here, man," Jeffers said. "You're a good shooter."

"Yeah, but my brother's in there," he said, nodding toward the dome. "Whatever the hell happens to us, I want to be able to see him again. Just one more time."

Jeffers put up his hands in surrender, then backpedaled into the bushes with the others.

Zeke tapped Hank on the shoulder, and the two men stepped toward the dome, their steps getting slower every inch along the way.

Roughly a hundred feet away, Hank could make out the features of the dome.

He saw a building that looked brand new compared to ruins that surrounded it. Its plexiglass roof arched high into the sky. Framed by the setting sun, it looked like a giant club waiting to swing down against the two guys.

"Thanks for volunteering to come with me," Hank said. "It'll help to have somebody who knows the place."

"Sure. But I can't imagine I'll be much help."

As they got closer, their words became hushed, almost muted.

Standing just a few feet away from what appeared to be a sealed front door, Hank swallowed hard. "I guess it's just a matter of time before they—"

Something speared him in his arm, bringing a sting to his bicep that felt like a million scorpions. Reaching down to find his balance, he saw the ground get blurry and shaky.

A heavy grunt came from Zeke as he, too, dropped the ground, hands splayed and torso quacking.

Hank fought for air but found none. His lungs squeezed shut as his vision faded to nothing. He could only hear footfalls getting closer and closer along with laughter and the clack of a gun getting cocked.

Then, he saw and heard nothing.

****

Hank woke up in a bed while a woman of twenty-five kept

a close watch over him. She looked like an overworked nurse, somebody who'd seen so much death and injury that life meant little to her.

Had she been dressed in anything but a grey sweatsuit and army boots, she might have been pretty. The crew cut also didn't help. "You still alive?" she asked him, a question seemingly driven only by curiosity.

"Huh?" Hank asked. He noticed he was also wearing an identical sweatsuit. It was tight around the waist and loose everywhere else.

"I just wanted to know if we had to start yet."

"Start what?"

"We're supposed to procreate."

"Excuse me?"

"Didn't they tell you?"

Hank rose to his feet and caught his breath. "Okay, let's start from the beginning. What do they do with people here?"

The woman shrugged. "Depends on the day. Monday through Thursday is lab day."

"What does that mean?"

"It means they take you through a whole bunch of tests. Not much fun. After a few days of that, your body just hurts. All that poking and prodding. Plus, all the weird pills they give you."

"Then Friday?"

The woman said, "Friday is a day of work. Lots of it. Mostly, they take you into the food lab and do food prep, cooking and what not."

"And weekends?"

"Saturday is sporting day."

"They let us play sports?" Hank asked.

The woman shook her head. "No, *they* play sports. They hunt people down and spear them. It gets ugly."

"And today is procreation day?"

The woman nodded sadly. "But don't get too excited." She pointed to a small, red rectangle between the ceiling and the wall. "They're watching everything. And if you don't do things right… they release some gases."

When the woman's face began to quiver, Hank took a seat next to her on the bed. He placed a warm hand on her shoulder, but she jerked away from it. "I probably shouldn't have said that" she said. "I'll get shocked for that."

"Can they hear us right now?"

"Probably. Honestly, I just don't care anymore. They can shock me and shock me. I can't possibly feel anything anymore… "

Hank studied her face, waiting for her to collapse into tears. But the collapse never came. She just stared straight ahead like a bored driver keeping her eyes on the road. Not sad. Not happy. Just alive. "So… are you ready?"

"Ready to procreate?" he asked.

"Of course."

"I guess so." He forced his face into a polite grin. "I'm Hank, by the way."

"I'm Julie," she said, not even bothering with eye contact.

"So… do we just get naked and…"

Julie shook her head. "No. They don't want us naked. The find that sort of thing creates… a bond. Or something like that. I forgot how they put it, but they want to make the whole thing as impersonal as possible."

"Well, if we're wearing clothes, how are we supposed to…" He studied the sweatsuit he'd been clad in, noticing a small flap in the front that buttoned down.

He said nothing but instead just stood up and locked his gaze on the red rectangle.

The woman said, "I wouldn't do that if I were—"

A jolt found Hank's chest, shoving him to the floor with a tightness in his chest and an inability to breathe. It was similar to the feeling he'd felt at the front door, but this time, the pain went away as swiftly as it came.

He climbed to his feet and took a seat on the bed, his breathing coming back and his lack of balance no longer sending him to the floor with an awkward lean.

The two of them sat in uneasy silence for a while as Julie's face twisted slightly. She looked like a psychic trying to see Hank's future.

When he started to speak, she quieted him with the lift of a hand. "They sent somebody."

"I'm sorry?"

"Outside," she went on. "They're coming. After a while, you're able to hear when somebody's—"

The room's door behind Hank's back swung open menacingly. Before he could turn to see what was happening, a shock came to his chest again, and he found himself in the grip of a strong guy.

The guy lifted him from the floor and put him across his shoulder like a sack of flour. He tried to fight to get free but couldn't. He bucked, kicked, bit, and clawed the assailant as he was carried down the hallway and Julie's expressionless face drifted further and further away.

Within seconds, they'd reached the door of a new room, and Hank found himself tossed onto the floor with minimum effort. He looked up and saw an ordinary office. A hard, plastic desk in the corner, carpeted floor, and file cabinet beside the door.

The musclebound man who'd carried him to the office stood next to a slender, bored-looking nerd seated on the edge of his desk. He leaned forward as if examining Hank for ticks. An uncomfortable silence followed and stayed there like a fog for at least a minute.

The nerdy man cleared his throat and spoke. "What is your story?" His voice was thin but oddly confident, like a cartoon mouse who'd been appointed general of an army.

"My story?" Hank asked, "I don't understand."

"Well… what the hell are doing here? You see, most people would have turned and ran at the sight of our compound here. But our security cameras indicated that you and your friend—who, by the way, was an escaped resident from here—you just… you walked up here. Didn't anybody tell you what we do here?"

"I was curious?"

The musclebound man let out a low chuckle, which slithered across the room.

The nerd stood and crouched over Hank's bruised body. "Okay, since you're so curious, I'll tell you what we do. Then, I'll show you, because as a resident, you'll be taken through everything."

The nerd returned to his desk and lifted his posture into a strong man's pose. "My name is Alfred, and I run things here. In fact, I've been running things here since before there was any 'here' to speak of."

"What does that mean?"

The muscled man answered for him. "It means he's the one who made all this happen." He gestured outside the window, indicating the wasteland the world had become.

"What my friend is saying is that I, with assistance from my underlings, manufactured the… apocalypse, if you will. We destroyed the world, so we could make it anew. And now, the next step in our process is to turn it into something that is better and stronger. To create a new species of humans, a race of people who won't make all those stupid mistakes humans are prone to."

"So, that's why you're doing all the experiments," Hank said.

"Of course," Alfred answered. "You didn't think we did all that just because we're a bunch of sick bastards, did you?"

Hank didn't answer. He just sat there and let all the information sink in.

"You're a very curious fellow," the nerd said. "And how do we feel about curiosity at the compound, eight-seventy-three?"

"We don't like it," the muscled man—apparently named eight-seventy-three—answered.

"That's right," Alfred said. "And when people strike us as especially curious, we feel the best way to feed that curiosity is a close-up look at what they're curious about."

"Huh?"

"What I'm saying, my friend, is you've got yourself a new job. You are my new assistant. The job will mostly consist of performing experiments on residents. You will also be tasked with the occasional execution of a resident who doesn't behave in exactly the way we'd like them to."

"What if I don't take the job?"

Alfred grinned. "You will take the job. Trust me. Our method of torture has been perfected to the point where we can say with complete certainty that you'd rather just do what we say than subject yourself to more."

Hank tried to stare the nerd down, summoning the courage to let this man know that he couldn't be broken. But it was getting him nowhere. And it occurred to him that maybe this job as Alfred's right-hand man could help the cause more than it could hurt it.

As an assistant, he'd have access to information that he ordinarily wouldn't. He could use this position to his advantage, and it might help save some lives. He stood with hands raised and said, "What's my first task?"

Alfred grinned. "Eight-seventy-three, take him to the lab."

****

With reluctant steps, Hank followed his guide to the lab. They stepped down a hallway that was spotless and eerily silent. The walls, floor, and ceiling were pure white, not a blemish to be seen.

Eight-seventy-three's face sported a smug grin from the moment they left the office, as if guarding a secret that he couldn't wait for Hank to discover. After a walk of roughly five minutes, they reached the lab. It was right behind two doors that pushed inward.

The lab looked like an ordinary doctor's laboratory, except for the lifeless bodies walking around. Each of the bodies wore grey sweatsuits and had faces fully lacking in expression of any kind. Hank's muscled guide led him to a steel gurney with a white sheet, then he turned to him and said, "We're gonna' start you out with a real easy one." He then spoke into an intercom on his wrist. "Send in forty-five-twelve."

Within a minute, a woman walked into the lab, her face as dead as everyone else's.

"Down," the muscled man ordered.

Without protest, the woman lay down on the gurney, face up and eyes obediently closed.

Eight-seventy-three turned to Hank and said, "You're gonna' remove this woman's spleen. Good luck." With a smile, he turned and left the lab, adding one more thing. "We'll be watching. And if things don't go well for her, they won't go well for you."

Now alone in the lab, Hank took a look around. He found red rectangles in the corners of the walls just as he had before. But on the other side of the lab, he saw something different, something that drew attention in that direction.

A small window gave him a glimpse of the outside. What he saw didn't bring a smile to his face. "Residents," as Alfred would have called them, were being worked hard. A muscled guard stood above them, whip in hand. He didn't use it, seemingly because he didn't need to. The people just tilled the earth, digging with shovels as if they understood they had no choice.

A few faces were familiar. Zeke was there, next to a slightly younger man who resembled him a little. Maybe it was his brother.

Julie was there, despondent and lifeless as ever. From a distance, she seemed to recognize his face in the window, but this didn't do anything to enliven her. She just shoveled and marched and shoveled like it was just another day in hell.

Hank noticed a door further down in the room, next to the hallway. From there, he tried to recall the layout of the building, retracing the steps eight-seventy-three took while carrying him to the office.

After a while, he could picture the layout of the dome. And he could visualize the path people would have to take to get out.

But it wouldn't be easy. He'd have to lead people out of the front door quickly and safely—a difficult task with the snipers aiming their shots at the front door.

Hank stared at the door leading into the yard and contemplated things, wondering how he could steer everyone from the yard to the front door.

It occurred to him that he had to simply do it, risk and all. There was no other way.

He made eye contact with Zeke. When recognition hit the bearded man's face, his face lit up. He knew it was time for action.

Hank took a look at the door and spotted a small button next to it, the kind you'd find on an elevator. He punched the button, and the door vertically flew open. Every face outside looked up. But nobody moved.

"Come on!" he screamed.

Zeke also screamed from the outside, urging the "residents" forward with slaps on the back and his manically waving arms. It didn't take much to move the herd forward. Together, they charged out of the yard and into the lab, steered by Hank's frantic motions.

The whip-wielding guard was trampled before he could find his footing, his weapon yanked from his grip by Zeke.

Once inside the lab, Hank moved the crowd down the hallway as they ignored the nagging blare of a siren. Together, they were close to the front door, no more than fifty feet away.

But the rattle of machine guns began before they got there. They desperately raced down the hallway as bodies fell and guards gave chase, guns blazing as they hit legs, ankles, torsos, and heads.

As the flood of bodies reached the front door and out of it, Hank yelled, "Down, everybody! Get down!"

The escapees ducked low as a series of shots came from the bushes, some hitting guards, a few hitting innocents. On his way out, Hank turned and spotted a familiar face among the armed guards. Alfred held a rifle, taking shots at the bushes as he tried to bring his guards into some kind of formation.

But it wasn't going to happen. There was too much chaos, and the sound of speeding bullets came whipping from too many directions. And when Alfred caught a bullet on the neck that sent him spinning to the ground like a windswept leaf, everybody there could sense it was over.

A few more shots came from the bushes, but the guards were surrendering now, arms aimed at the sky as they gathered around their lifeless leader. Their eyes seemed full of contempt for his dead body. As if they, too, were prisoners. Maybe they were.

Hank lifted a hand to gesture for the snipers to stop firing. He took cautious steps back inside to check on the carnage. Several "residents" had been killed, and one of them had a familiar face. "Zeke," he said softly, looking at the big man's now bloodied face, his eyes peacefully shut.

A voice from behind startled Hank. "Did you know my brother?"

The guy's eyes were watery, his face threatening to buckle into sobs.

Hank nodded. "I sure did." He stood to give the guy a hug, then said to him, "You know why he volunteered to come back in here?"

He shook his head.

"I'll tell you all about it," Hank said. "But only if you promise to tell me all about what kind of guy he was before."

"It's a deal."

The gang gathered around now, gazing at the carnage and the survivors. When he spotted the smile on an unlikely face, Hank had a feeling he'd done the right thing.

Julie stepped closer to him; arms wide as she came in for a hug. "This place isn't home anymore," she said. "I never thought I'd say that."

Hank stepped back and watched all the joy unfolding amidst all the tragedy. He didn't know what the next step was, how everybody would get by in what the world had now become. All he knew was that they were free. And that was a good place to start.

DESPERATE TIMES

Helen was running late. With Andy getting out of school soon, she had to get there in ten minutes to get back in time for the book club meeting, then make sure dinner was done.

That was why she didn't even notice the note at first.

It sat there on her windshield, crumpled up, words scribbled out in a violent shade of red.

After noticing it, she got out of her seat with a sigh and scooped it into her pocket without even reading it. Who had time? Andy was waiting. Her cellphone was ringing, and some jerk was leaning on his horn behind her.

She took off, breathing for what felt like the first time in hours and answering her cell phone.

"Yeah?"

"What time are you getting here?" a shrill voice demanded.

With all the chaos swimming in her head, she wasn't sure who it was initially.

The voice was too high to be her husband's. It wasn't Andy because he didn't have a cell phone yet—despite his incessant screeching for one. She paused, flicking through her mental rolodex.

"Monica!"

"Yes, didn't you say you'd be here at 5:30?"

"My God, I'm so sorry. I forgot you needed me to watch the ranch today. I am so, so sorry."

Her friends Monica and Tate owned a horse ranch. They needed her to watch it for a few days while they took a vacation.

"No worries, long as you get here in the next half-hour we can still make our flight."

"Half-hour, huh? Well, I'll see what I can do."

"Look, if it's too much of a bother…"

"No, no. I said I'd be there, and I will. I promise."

"Great, see you soon."

"Bye, Monica."

Helen hung up and breathed out a massive sigh.

She stopped at a streetlight and stared at the sky, wondering why everything in the world had happened at exactly the same time. Andy getting picked up from school. Rex getting back from the airport. Monica and Tate needing her at the ranch. Why?

For a split second, she floated into a dream, where she lived a less cluttered life, the kind she wanted as a teenager. A big house, maybe a mansion. Kids, but not too many. A husband who understood and, of course, a masseuse always on call.

A loud, angry horn coming from the car behind her jolted her back to reality. The light had changed.

She pulled up to the school, hoping Andy was waiting out front where he was supposed to be so she wouldn't have to sit there in the middle of the street and endure a barrage of curse words from those who had to wait behind her.

It turned out that Andy was there, but he was taking his time getting to the car. He traded action figures with a friend and giggled over something. Helen tried to get him moving with a honk of her horn.

With nothing to do but wait, she tugged the note from her pocket and read it.

We have Rex.

Will kill him if you call anybody. The police or anybody else.

This is no joke.

Will reach out with further details about how you can save him.

Her body went still and numb. This couldn't be happening.

The door's sudden opening startled her.

"Hi, Mom!"

Helen tried to breathe, move, anything. The note slipped from her fingers to the floor.

"Mom?"

****

This had to be a joke, maybe a cruel one. But it couldn't be real.

Rex was kidnapped? How was this possible? Who would do this? Why?

These were the thoughts that slashed through her brain on the car ride home.

She wanted to go to the police and scream for help. *But what if they hurt him? Or killed him?*

"Mom, are you okay?" Andy asked.

She said nothing, stroking his hair with her hand and staring straight ahead, trying not to look suspicious.

"Why is your hand shaking?" her son asked.

She swallowed hard and forced out words. "Andy, I'm going to drop you off at your friend Jeff's house." She checked his face for a reaction.

He wrinkled his brow. "Why? Is something wrong?"

"Because I said so. Stop asking questions." She snapped back at him, and despite feeling bad about her attitude, she didn't apologize. She couldn't afford to encourage his curiosity.

The wrinkle remained as she drove him to his friend's house. Thankfully, he remained silent as well.

She managed to get home despite trembling fingers and thoughts that raced all over the place. The walk up the driveway and inside seemed to take forever. After unlocking the door, she opened it slowly.

The house looked normal, but that didn't stop her from feeling violated. Somebody was watching her, ready to strike.

Helen took slow, cautious steps across the kitchen linoleum, eyes darting from the windows to the bathroom door to the living room. "Hello?"

Her cell rang, nearly sending her wired body crashing to the floor.

She answered on the first ring, her voice breathy and fragile. "Hello?"

"What are you going to do?"

She slammed her eyes shut, tried to think. *Who is this?*

It was a woman's voice, one she recognized. "Monica!"

"Look, if you can't do it, you can't do it. No big deal."

There was so much she wanted to say. She wanted—needed—to cry out for help. She wanted Monica to call the police, see if they could help find out where Rex was.

But that was a risky move.

The note said don't tell anyone.

Helen took a deep breath. "This is a bad day, Monica. Very bad."

"Hey, it's okay. But if things get better and you can make it, there's an 8:45 we can catch. So, if you can be here at 8, that'd be terrific."

Helen stood there in the kitchen, frozen, eyes still darting around her deceptively quiet home.

Monica went on, a trace of annoyance in her voice. "Okay... so if we don't hear from you by 8, we'll try to get somebody else. So... goodbye?"

Helen said nothing. She slowly tucked the cell back into her purse.

Then, she pulled it out again, brought it to her ear. Maybe there was a way to notify the police without the kidnappers knowing what was happening.

She started dialing, then she stopped.

The doorbell rang.

****

Standing at the doorway, Dennis McCoy had way too many thoughts racing through his head.

Every visit to Rex's house raised troubling memories, and this trip was no exception.

In his head, he rehearsed what he'd say to Helen if she started asking questions. He was dropping off a package for her husband, probably some kind of power tool or something, no need to take a look.

God only knew how she'd react if she took a look.

When Helen didn't answer, he rang the doorbell a second time, catching a glimpse of her standing in the kitchen, cell phone in her hand. She was a sweet lady, probably didn't suspect a thing about her husband's past—or his present. McCoy's body shook with guilt whenever he visited her.

After a third ring, he saw her turn and look toward the door. But she didn't walk toward it.

That phone call must have been important, maybe stressful. Her eyes seemed wide with panic, even from this distance.

He waved at her through the side window, smiling. No way

could he just leave the package on the front steps. Returning home with it and coming back later was also not an option. Rex needed it immediately.

McCoy wondered if Helen ever suspected anything. She knew her husband was a combat veteran; probably even knew he'd killed some people.

But did she have any idea what Rex's real life looked like after his time in the Special Forces? Probably not.

They'd been sworn to secrecy, and Rex wasn't the kind of guy to violate that oath—even with his own wife.

He started to reach out for a fourth ring but then noticed her stepping toward the door, cellphone now tucked back into her purse.

He heard the locks coming undone, but it seemed to take forever for the door to open. There was a clumsiness in her hands that seemed common in nervous people. He recognized it from work.

The door swung open. She cleared her throat and spoke. "Hi, Dennis," she said, voice higher pitched than usual. "Is that for Rex?"

"Sure is."

She didn't move or speak. Something about her shaky gasps of breath told him she was in trouble, needed help.

"You okay, Helen?"

She nodded, trying to collect herself. Without a word, she reached for the package, her lips stretched tight like somebody holding back tears.

But McCoy got a sense that it wouldn't be a good idea to hand over the package. Maybe her odd demeanor came from suspicion. Maybe she'd open it and take a look after he took off. That would be a huge problem. It would put her at risk.

"You know, maybe I'll just wait until Rex comes back if you don't mind," he said. "This is kind of important, and I—"

"No!" she yelled; her voice uneven, shaky. She composed herself by clearing her throat. "I just mean... it may be a while before he gets back, so... I don't want to make you wait any longer than you'd like to. That's all."

Her words were reassuring, but her body language told a different tale. He'd seen this kind of panic before. He'd seen it in people who owed the wrong person a giant sum of money and were facing death.

He leaned in closer. "You sure you're okay?"

She stared at him, eyes shaky and desperate, unable to push words from her mouth. She gave her head a subtle shake to say "no." It was as if she was trying to pass on a code, trying to keep her conversation a secret. Through quivering lips, she mouthed the words, *I can't tell you.*

A million grim possibilities scampered through McCoy's head. Without words, he stepped inside, eyes scanning the living room, the kitchen, the hallway to the bedrooms. Helen backpedaled as if afraid of him.

He took a few more steps past her as she froze in place. He ducked his hand into his breast pocket but didn't pull the gun out yet.

A soft whimper came from Helen, and he turned to face her. Words still failed her, but there was no doubt that she was panicked. Behind her, he caught a reflection of something metallic, something that moved a little. But he was careful not to react to it just yet.

Eyes still locked on whatever it was, he said to Helen, "You just make sure Rex gets this package and I'll be back later."

Helen seemed on the verge of collapse, her breathing sounding like an idle engine.

He focused more on the shiny item in the distance, watching it edge to a slightly higher angle, a head now coming into focus.

He had to act now.

"Get down!" He shouted, shoving her to the carpet, then spinning to the target, his gun out and firing twice.

He heard shots from the kitchen, then a low groan that sounded like a tire losing air. Helen's screams filled the living room as he raced toward the target, his body flat on the kitchen floor, arms outstretched and rifle across his belly.

Once in the kitchen, McCoy slowed down, took a glance at the target, gun trained on him, even though he was clearly no longer a threat. He crept to the kitchen's rear, his gun still out and going from one space to another.

When it seemed like there was nobody else there, he returned to the target, shouting, "You okay, Helen?"

"I'm... well... I guess so."

"What's that mean?"

"It means I guess so. I don't know what okay is supposed to feel like after something like that."

He scanned the target's body. He was clad in army fatigues, boots a little tattered—maybe battle-worn—hair cropped short. "Right now, all that matters is you're alive."

He stepped back toward her, then stooped to better inspect her prone body. "The note!" she screamed. "There was a note!"

With shaky hands, she reached into her purse and pulled out a piece of paper with words written in red ink. "I got this on my windshield."

McCoy studied her face, wondering what he should tell her.

"Should we call the police?" she asked.

"Absolutely not," he answered. "Is the boy—what was his name again—is he safe?"

"Andy, and, yeah, I brought him to a friend's house when I got the note." Another wave of worry reached her face. "You don't think they could have gotten him there!" She yanked out her cellphone and frantically dialed.

"He's probably fine, but I suppose it wouldn't hurt to check."

She whimpered through a few questions about her son, then profusely thanked whoever it was she was talking to and hung up. "Yes, he's fine, but I am so scared right now. For Andy, for Rex..."

Helen seemed to be searching for answers that McCoy didn't have. All he knew was that it wasn't a good idea to be in that house anymore. "Let's get out of here," he told her.

****

While McCoy took care of the situation—disposing of the body, cleaning the scene—Helen watched him with alert and disturbed eyes. She didn't ask questions, but McCoy knew she must have had many. He clearly looked like somebody who'd done this kind of thing before. And for good reason.

Once finished with the clean-up, he cracked opened the door, scanned the scene quickly, then grabbed her by the arm, gun at his hip.

The risk of another gunman seemed minimal, but this was not the time to be spotted by a nosy neighbor. So, they stayed in a crouch and waited for absolute quiet.

Once he was satisfied with the silence, he said, "Okay, we're going to the car, nice and normal. Do not panic. Anything out of the ordinary happens, let me handle it. Is that clear?"

She nodded.

"Let's go." Just as planned, they stepped to the car, trying to walk like normal. Helen did her best to hide the twitch on her face and her fidgety hands.

Once in the car, she unloaded a breath, then asked, "Will you please tell me what all this is about?"

"I'll do my best," he said. "But understand that under ordinary circumstances, I would not be able to tell you any of this."

He started his car up and took off.

"So... you know where my husband is?"

"I have a pretty good guess, yes."

"Is he safe?"

"I wish I could answer that, ma'am. All I can tell you is how he got where he is now. And for that, I'm going to have to tell you some things you may not want to hear."

She released a nervous titter. "Wonderful. Like the news so far hasn't been bad enough."

While driving to I-94, he kept his eyes busy, checking both mirrors for surprise visitors. "First, let me ask you," he said, "What do you know about Rex's career?"

She turned again as if puzzled by the question. "His career? Well... he was in the army, Special Forces. And I know that involved lots of top-secret work. You don't think this has anything to do with that, do you?"

He tried to find the words, but before he could, she spat out more. "I mean, that was years ago. Why would somebody from ten, eleven years ago, from some combat mission that's over, why would they want to kidnap him? Or kill him?"

McCoy took a deep breath. "Actually, ma'am, I'm afraid this is about something more recent."

"More recent? But he hasn't been in the army in years!"

"True. But I'm afraid there's some things about his life after the Special Forces that... well, may be news to you."

Helen buried her face in her hands as if shielding herself from blows. After slowly pulling her face back up, she asked another question. "Where are we going?"

"I don't know, ma'am. I suppose I should ask you: is there some kind of safe house we can go to?"

"Safe house? You mean a place where nobody wants to kill me?"

"That's the gist of it, yes."

"How about a ranch?"

"Ma'am?"

"This couple, these friends of mine, need somebody to watch their ranch. They have horses. I guess I would be safe there."

"Perfect."

"I can't believe this is happening," she said, eyes straight ahead, face still.

An uneasy silence fell. McCoy broke the silence by asking for the address.

She gave it, her voice growing weaker with every syllable.

"The first thing you need to know," McCoy said, "is that I take the blame for the choices your husband made. Rex was a good man, a wonderful, loyal soldier. I went and dragged him into things he probably regrets. I would not blame you at all for being angry with me."

"Can you please just tell me what I need to know," she said. "I've had enough suspense today."

He cleared his throat, wondering where to start.

****

The two men ran into each other at Hervey's, a sports bar at the mall. One of those annoyingly loud places with way more TV screens that anyone could possibly need.

With the game over, the crowd began to thin, and McCoy thought he recognized a guy alone in the booth. He stared at the table beneath him, his face looking weirdly blank.

McCoy stepped over, took a seat. "Hey, hey! That's a pretty long face for a man whose team just won in overtime."

Rex looked up, a smile creeping onto his face. "McCoy? Jesus God, it's been a while! Four, five years?"

"Something like that. I know it's been too long. The hell has been keeping you busy these days?"

Rex shrugged. "You know. Wife, new baby. A job until a few

weeks ago."

"One of those big corporate layoffs? Yeah, lots of that crap going on these days."

Rex gave him sad eyes and shook his head. "No, not that. This job I lost on my own."

McCoy tried to find a delicate way to ask the question. "You, uh… having problems again?"

He nodded.

"You can get help, you know. There's no shame in it."

Without smiling, Rex laughed a little. "Easy for you to say. Besides, is there really help?"

"Of course there is. There are therapists and what not. They got a name for it and a treatment plan. It's not like back in the day, when they'd just say that you're shellshocked. They can help you."

Rex shook his head slowly, eyes still on the table. "Right now what I need is a job."

McCoy said nothing. This was a sore spot, a place he wasn't ready to go.

Looking up for the first time, Rex turned and met his gaze almost bravely. "You got a job?"

"Kind of."

"The hell does that mean? How do you kind of have a job?"

"I got something happening, but this conversation is about you."

"Yes, it's about what I need. And what I need is a job. Something to take me out of my head."

McCoy stared at him, tried not to look like he was pitying his friend. "There's your pension."

Rex's pulled his lips back tightly, holding something back, probably tears. "You haven't heard, have you?"

"Heard what?"

"It's a long story, but basically, they decided my actions were 'not honorable.'"

McCoy slammed a fist to the table. "I can't believe it."

"I can. We knew we were acting on our own, not under orders. We were risking everything, and that's what happens when you risk everything."

"Look, maybe there's somewhere you can go for money."

"No," he said, firm like a bullet to the forehead. "If I sit around the rest of my life on welfare, I don't know what I'd do. Seriously, I might just do a self-serve."

"Don't talk like that."

"I'm being honest. I'd take myself out before being a welfare case. Where did you find work?"

McCoy looked around, checking for eavesdroppers. "This goes nowhere, okay?"

"Of course."

"There's a guy in town, a dealer."

"Drug dealer?" Rex asked, his voice low.

After another quick glance around, McCoy nodded. "He needed muscle, somebody to enforce things."

Rex managed a half-smile. "He still need it?"

"You don't want to get involved. Trust me. It's illegal. You've got a family. They need you at home, not in jail."

"What do you do, day to day?"

McCoy shrugged. "Mostly collect people's debt."

"Ever had to…" Rex made a gun firing gesture.

McCoy shook his head. "Eight months, and nothing like that so far."

"Sounds pretty easy."

"Like I said. So far. Somebody gets out of line, doesn't want to pay, waits for you in the front yard with a shotgun, the job duties may change."

"Seriously McCoy, after all the stuff we did—eight years of it—you think I couldn't handle that?"

"Sure you could, but you don't want to. What you want is to go home, retire from anything involving firearms. Anything involving shooting, killing. You want a nice boring life, football on Sunday, PTA meetings, wife dragging you to cocktail parties. You want what I had before Carole left."

Rex brought his eyes back to the table. "It's too late for that. There's no other life for me. Do you get that?"

McCoy said nothing. But he understood exactly what Rex meant.

Working special forces took something from you, made you a different kind of guy. It was as if you had to sacrifice your soul. Even before Carole took off with the kids, McCoy knew he'd never be the same guy. Something was missing and always would be.

Rex looked at him again. "Just give me the guy's number. Let me figure it out for myself."

His friend nodded weakly, then dug a pen from his breast pocket and scribbled the number on a napkin. When he slid the napkin to Rex, he nodded. He could see a faint glow on his face. It wasn't joy exactly, but something more serious.

"I appreciate this," he said, tucking the napkin in his pocket. After a deep exhale, he said. "I better be getting home now."

They stood and stared at each other long and hard. Rex seemed to need a hug, but a handshake was probably all they could handle. Any more than that, and they'd turn into a couple guys crying in public.

****

McCoy lifted his eyes off the road just long enough to read Helen's face. Her expression had landed somewhere between dejection and anger.

"I'm really sorry," he said. "I never would have gotten him into any of that if there was any kind of plan B for him."

She put her hands on the dashboard, reaching for emotional balance. She turned her face away.

"You okay?" he asked.

"No, I'm not okay." She brought her eyes back to him. "So, that's why he got abducted? He got snared into that world, that… drug world?"

"It's a little more complicated than that," McCoy said. "He made the mistake of letting Niko know he was a sniper."

"Niko?"

"He's the dealer. Greek guy. He found out Rex was a sniper, and he was called in for duty that was a lot more intense than the stuff I was doing—the stuff he thought he would be doing. Now, Niko's thinking Rex is a hired hand, somebody to call when he needs somebody put down."

Helen gasped, her breath growing heavy, sounding like a cheap fan. McCoy tried to comfort her with a hand on her shoulder, but she pulled away from it. "He kills people? That's what my husband does for a living?"

"I'm sorry."

She buried her face in her hands without making a sound. She looked like a frightened child braced for a beating.

"Helen, these were really bad people, all of them. Lowlifes who owed Niko money. Some were guys who tried to kill Niko."

She looked up from her hands, sent a sad face to McCoy. "He kills people?" she repeated, voice frail.

"As far as him getting abducted… that's a little more complicated. And it's kind of my fault."

"Of course it was your fault. It was all your fault. You didn't have to bring him into this world."

McCoy said nothing. He drove, eyes straight ahead because he didn't want Helen's distraught face to remind him of what he'd done. "We're low on gas. You know where we can get some?"

She took forever to answer, then finally said, "Keep straight ahead and take a left when we get to that mall up ahead."

The gas station was tiny, a place they could maintain their low profiles. Nobody there to ask questions.

But pulling up to the pump, he noticed a red van that seemed to be driving too slowly around the back of the station. It was the kind of thing most people would never have thought twice about, but after years in the special forces, then more time as an enforcer in the drug world, he couldn't *not* notice it if he tried.

He didn't move or say anything at first. He just scanned the landscape using only his peripheral vision.

He noticed a young teenage girl in the station, eyes locked on her cellphone laying on the counter as she tied her hair in a bun. Except for the occasional passing car—all doing at least eighty— there was nobody else.

Without moving, he addressed Helen. "Here's what we're going to do: you're going to duck down into your seat—as far as you can go. Just make sure the top of your head is no higher than the dashboard."

"What?"

"Helen, just do it. Duck down. Now."

She dropped in her seat slowly, eyes wide, lips pulled tight.

"Okay. I'm going to be gone for a second, and you're going to stay right there. Do you understand me?"

"Yes," she said, her voice a barely audible gasp.

McCoy casually left the car, eyes down as he pretended to look at his cellphone. He stepped into the gas station, checking the landscape from the side as he approached the counter. "You got a bathroom?" he asked the girl.

Without looking up or speaking, she reached to her left and pulled down a big metal spoon with a key attached, then pointed just past the stack of potato chips.

He walked in. After locking the door behind him, he opened the window and jumped out.

With his gun out, he crept through the weeds just behind the gas station and checked the parking lot. The red van was there, but nobody was in the driver's seat.

The space by the parking lot was lined with waist-high weeds, providing a perfect sniper's nest fifty feet from the target. McCoy couldn't see anybody there, but he counted on somebody showing up.

He crouched there and waited. He didn't have to wait long.

The crown of a black cap showed itself. A turret jutted out of the weeds.

He trained his sig Sauer on the cap, body tucked lower to make sure nobody in the van could see him.

He fired two shots, then watched as the black cap and the turret dropped out of view. The van didn't move, which probably meant there was nobody else to take care of.

He slipped back into the bathroom window, then raced outside the bathroom in time to hear a pair of high-pitched voices, wailing in horror.

After tossing the key and the spoon on the now unmanned counter, he ran outside, finding the source of the two screams. Helen, seated in the car with the door open, and the teenaged attendant both pointed at an area in the weeds.

"What the hell was that sound?" McCoy yelled.

Breathless, the attendant turned to him, still pointing at the weeds. "Nobody knows, it just kind of came from over there in that parking lot, I swear to God! I'm gonna call the cops just to be sure, but it's probably nothing."

"Sure was loud, whatever it was," McCoy said, casually strolling to the side of the car to pump gas. The teenager went back inside.

Helen looked up at him, no words spoken, but her eyes were asking for answers.

"I told you to stay down," he whispered.

"I'm sorry. I'm so scarred right now."

****

After leaving the gas station, he asked. "Are we going the right way?"

"Yes." She spoke in a voice that was firmer now, more laced with anger than sadness. "We're about two miles away. About a half a mile from the billboard you'll see on your left."

He nodded and kept driving. "And your friends are expecting you?"

"Yes. I'm supposed to be watching the ranch for the weekend, taking care of the horses while they're gone. Will we be safe there?"

"We should be?"

"But you're not sure?"

"Helen, I'm going to do the best I can to make sure you're safe and to make sure we get Rex back. That's the only thing I can promise."

There was more silence before they reached the ranch, a large, sprawling estate isolated from everything with several acres lined with greenery and a wooden fence. McCoy regarded the scenery as good news. It would be difficult for anyone to sneak up on them.

He stopped the car about a half mile before getting there.

"Okay, here's what we're going to do. Having me tag along might be a little too much for you to explain to your friends, so if they ask, I'm just driving you here. If they ask why, make something up, anything. I'm going to scan the periphery, make sure we're safe, then I'll be there. Got it?"

She nodded, then left the car and walked toward the ranch, her limbs looking stiff. As he looked down, checking his gun, McCoy shook his head. He always hated the thought of innocent people getting caught up in the game. And possibly getting killed because of it.

****

Helen took a deep breath as she trudged forward, eyes racing around like gnats at a barbecue. This was beyond scary. Not knowing what was happening to Rex and not knowing where she or her son were next in line brought a rattle to her limbs. She wanted to collapse into a corner, soaking herself in tears. But there was no corner to collapse into.

The door swung open before she could reach for the doorbell.

Monica's eyes stretched wide like she'd spotted a corpse on her porch. "Helen? Are you okay?"

Her husband's head sprang up behind her, his face also locked in a surprised gaze. "What happened?"

Helen swallowed hard and lifted her lips into a grin. "I'm fine. Just stressed out, that's all."

The couple exchanged glances, silently wondering if the other one bought her excuse. Monica said, "Okay, we're all packed and ready to take off. You know how to handle the horses, right? We've shown you everything before."

"Yes, I'm fine."

With their bags already at the door, the couple darted past her and to the driveway. "Give us a call if you need anything!"

Helen stood there and watched them get into the car, knowing all she had to do was tell them that everything wasn't okay. They were right there.

But she knew it was risky. She believed whoever wrote that note. And she believed Rex's friend, McCoy.

So, she stood there and watched the couple's grey minivan disappear into the night. After that, she spun in a slow circle, not seeing anyone. Not McCoy or anyone else.

She stepped into the open door and pulled out her cellphone, dialing the first few numbers of Andy's friend's house. If nothing else, she needed to know her son was safe. But she didn't get past the first three numbers before a bark came from behind. "Do not call anybody!"

Helen turned and spotted McCoy racing towards her and snatching the cell from her hand. "You have no idea how easy it would be for somebody to find your location like that," he said. "Really bad idea!"

Pulse racing with rage, she tried to take the phone back, but he grabbed her arms, then tucked it into his pocket. "Helen, we need to be very careful."

She exploded. "And I need to know if my son is safe!"

He gave her a soft nod, then spoke as if addressing a mental patient reluctant to take her meds. "Helen, these people are deadly. You have no idea who you're dealing with. Your only hope is to do exactly as they say."

"And… if I do what they say, my family will be safe."

He paused, lips tight, holding back the bad news. "I can't promise you that. But I can promise that if you can't keep your emotions in check, you and your family are not going to make it. I hate to be blunt about it, but if they feel like they have to, they will kill you all."

Helen sent her eyes away, trying to hold back a breakdown. "I'm scared," she whimpered.

He nodded, probably wanting to say, 'I am, too.'

But instead, he said, "I'll stand watch while you go get some sleep."

Her eyes sent spears into his own. "You honestly think I can sleep with all this happening?"

He nodded again but seemed out of words. "Whatever you do, just make sure you stay inside unless I give you the okay. I'll be standing watch. Anything happens, let me know."

He took off out of the back door, and Helen stayed in the center of the room, arms crossed, body motionless. Once McCoy took off, not a single sound from outside intruded into the space. No traffic. No planes. No neighbors with loud radios on their backyard decks, the kind that used to drive her insane.

Never before had silence been so frightening.

****

Daylight took forever to reach her.

She didn't sleep at all, didn't even leave the spot in the living room. She only gave her legs a rest and took a seat after McCoy came inside to tell her everything was clear outside.

She remained motionless, eyes still busy, while he went to the kitchen to find some breakfast. "Lots of stuff here!" he shouted. "Eggs, sausage. Blueberry pancakes. Not the good kind, the kind you have to microwave, but you have to eat something, right?"

Helen didn't answer, even as he stepped out of the kitchen and took a seat next to her with two plates of eggs and sausage links.

"There's orange juice in there, too, if you want some."

"I'm not hungry."

"You sure? You haven't eaten in all the time I've been—"

"I'm not hungry."

He nodded silently, knowing when it was time to stop asking questions.

But soon after scarfing down his eggs, he was at it again. "You know, I've got an extra gun on me. I really think it'd be a good idea if I schooled you in how to use it. I mean, God forbid you have to, but just to be on the safe side, I think I should show you the basics, make sure nobody can get in here and… you know, cause some problems." He made eye contact with her, waiting for a reply.

She didn't have the kind of answer he was waiting for. "Why has my husband been abducted?"

"It's a long story."

"We've got time. It doesn't look like we're going anywhere for a while."

He leaned back in his chair and sighed. "It's kind of my fault."

"Excuse me?"

McCoy said, "I was given a mission I wasn't comfortable with. It involved innocent people."

"If we get out of this thing alive, I don't ever want to see you again."

His face slackened. "Look, I can understand you'd be a little upset—"

"No, you don't understand. You have no idea how angry I am at you. For bringing my husband into this dangerous world that has now put my family at risk."

"Helen, slow down. Please."

Teeth clenched and eyes narrowed, she aimed her rage at somewhere else in the room and remained silent.

He stood up and backpedaled away. "I'll be outside, doing a little target practice. If you want to join me, I'll—"

She silenced him with a baleful stare.

And the conversation was over.

****

For nearly an hour, Helen watched McCoy take shots at bales of hay with newspaper tied around them. It almost felt like staring at a man who was guilty of murdering her husband. It was, after all, his fault that Rex got roped into this world.

For the first few minutes, she'd flinch at every shot. Something about that sharp metallic slap that jabbed her ear drum reminded her of dangers she didn't want to be reminded of.

Not that she'd ever been a fan of guns.

Simply knowing her husband had been a combat veteran was enough to make her uneasy. She intentionally asked him not to share details of his battles. But soon, the details came gushing out anyway—mostly in the form of his nightmares. He'd wake up screaming in the late hours of the night, gripping his pillow like a child taking a beating, his throat hoarse from screams, his knees tucked to his chest. It hurt her when she saw him like that.

After a while, it became an almost nightly occurrence. She begged him to get help, and he insisted there was no way he could be helped. He'd simply have to tough it out and learn to live with it.

That was about a decade ago.

Watching McCoy shoot at the bales of hay was too much to take. So, she brought it to an end by stepping out of the screen door and walking over to him, arms folded, face blank.

He turned when he heard her approach. "I'm sorry. Was this bothering you?"

She shook her head. "You said something about having a spare gun?"

"I'm sorry?"

She swallowed hard and delivered a difficult series of words. "I figure as long as there's danger out there, I might as well do what I can to make myself safe."

His eyes warmed as if surprised to hear it. A smile crawled onto his face. "Sure, let me get that for you..." he placed a foot on top of the horse's trough and lifted his pant leg to reveal a small pistol strapped to his ankle. He unstrapped it, pointed it at the ground and gestured for her to take a look as he opened the magazine.

McCoy gave her a thirty-minute crash course in gun handling and gun shooting.

The lessons set her on edge, but none of her squeamishness slowed down her desire to learn more.

He taught her how to load the magazine, where to point it while doing so, and how to hold the gun with a firm grip and steady stance before firing.

It took a while for her to hit the bale of air a mere twenty feet in front of her, but she got there after a while, pleasing herself and her instructor as well.

After about ten minutes of consistently reaching the target, he said, "Nice work. Let's take a break."

She nodded, smiling at him for the first time since he came to her door a day earlier. "I think our friends need to be checked on," she said, nodding toward the horse stable.

Monica and Tate had three horses in a stable that held as many as ten. On Helen's first trip there, she was stunned by how sleek and clean the place looked. It looked like the equestrian version of a helicopter's parent's nursery.

"Handsome little fella, isn't he?" McCoy said about the dark brown Arabian named Pepper.

"Sure," Helen answered. "Not the easiest guy to ride, though. Trust me on that."

As McCoy stroked Pepper's mane, he turned to Helen and asked, "You suppose they need to be taken out for a ride?"

"They'd love it. But I suppose you better start with Lucy first. Pepper can be a little—"

He lifted his hand to motion for quiet, keeping his face eerily still.

"What?" she whispered.

He put a finger to his lips, eyes slowly creeping from left to right. He lifted the gun from his holster, loaded it, and held it at his hip, then leaned over and brought his lips to her ear. "I heard somebody circling this place slowly. I could be worrying over nothing, but just to be safe, you go inside, find a place to hide—a closet, maybe, or under a bed—stay there until you hear something from me."

When she registered his words, Helen froze, her body stubbornly refusing to obey.

With an urgent jerk of his head, McCoy gestured her inside.

She took a deep breath and followed his order. Before she got there, he grabbed her by the shoulder and turned her, then mouthed the words *hold onto your gun—just in case.*

Helen took off slowly, hearing his footfalls behind her.

When she reached the hallway, her steps grew slower, more cautious. It was all she could do to keep the gun from slipping out of her hand to the hardwood floor.

Her eyes swept the landscape, racing from side-to-side with the steady, locked rhythm of busy windshield wipers. She found a closet near the kitchen and tucked herself inside, slowly closing the door behind her.

The last image she saw before being swallowed by the dark was McCoy's stern face as he tiptoed to the front door, gun now raised to his chest.

Helen enveloped her head into her arms, the pistol's barrel cold against her temple until she yanked it away frightened.

She waited, not entirely sure what she was waiting for.

A buzz in her back pocket rattled her, sending the gun tumbling to the closet floor. Luckily, it landed on a parka that had fallen and didn't make a sound.

Helen tried to still her trembling arms with a deep breath. When that didn't work, she tried a second one, then reached into her back pocket and pulled out her cell.

It was a text from her husband.

I'm alive and well. For now.

They've got me in the car outside.

Rex.

A gasp flew from Helen's mouth. She clamped it shut as her breath thundered from her lungs.

Ideas and thoughts circled around her head like fireflies.

Should I tell McCoy something? Or should I just wait?

A gun shot rang from the front door, followed by two more. Eyes now wide and her body shaking, she rearranged the gun in her hand—just in case.

Silence followed for a few seconds, then a car engine in front roared to life. Fast footsteps pounded into room from the front door, getting closer to the closet. They were loud, heavy, urgent.

The door swung open with an ominous creak. McCoy stood there, breathless, tucking his gun away. "I don't know what happened, but somebody knows where we are. So, we better get you out of here!"

She gathered her breath, then answered, "They have Rex!"

"What?"

"In the car," she said, voice cracking and strained. She lifted her cell and showed him, holding her trembling arm at the wrist so he could see the text.

"I'm going after him!" he said, yanking her to the feet and running with her to the front door. "And I don't want to leave you here alone with them knowing you're here!"

They sprinted to the car as a black van sped away down a dusty road, maybe a hundred or a hundred and fifty feet ahead of them.

He put her in the back, then jumped into the driver's seat. "Duck down as far as you can! Shots *will* be exchanged!"

The car took off, moving fast enough to shove Helen's unprepared body into the seat behind her.

"You still got your gun?" he asked.

"Um... I... " In the rush of the moment, she wasn't sure. So, she jabbed hand into her pocket until she felt metal. "Yes! Um, are we going to need it?"

"I hope not," she said, voice hushed as if really talking to himself.

"Me too," she said, unable to brace her body as the car took sharp turns at what felt like at least ninety miles an hour. She didn't dare lift her head to see the road before them, but she imagined what was happening. She pictured them closing in on the black van. They had to be gaining ground with how fast they were moving.

The sounds of the road got louder and loaded with bumps and rattles. It seemed they were moving to an abandoned area, maybe not even on the road anymore.

A gun shot rang out of the driver side window, probably McCoy shooting at the van, but with everything unfolding so quickly and chaotically, Helen couldn't be sure. She coiled her body into a tight ball between the seat in front of her and one behind her.

The car sent her crashing back and forth like a pinball. Her head thumped against the hard door and the pistol's barrel pushed into the soft cushion of the seat behind her.

Another gunshot sounded as the screech of tires filled her ears. Tiny pellets of stone thudded against the car like a million drunk snare drummers.

The car spun for what seemed like a minute, tires screeching, breaks creaking as McCoy's foot pumped hard against the pedal.

Then came the crash of metal on metal, loud enough to make her scream and drop the gun. The car spun more, sideways this time, as shattered glass rained into her hair and she thumped back and forth, body coming undone, limbs flying everywhere.

The car found stillness as a long, low grunt came from McCoy.

Helen found her body spread lengthwise along the space between the car's front seats and the back seats. With a groan, she lifted herself up and gazed out of the windshield. The van was turned on its side, as one silhouette dragged another by manacles toward an old, abandoned factory.

It was Rex being dragged away, his hands shackled, his body limp and covered with blood.

A throaty grunt brought her attention back to the car. McCoy turned, blood coming from his mouth, eyes straining to stay open. "I... can't help him," he said with major effort.

His arm was sliced at the shoulder. It lay limp at his side.

"What do we do?" she asked.

"Nothing... we can do," he said. "They got him. They... won."

The two silhouettes were now gone. A haunting silence surrounded her.

A buzz came from her pocket, nearly sending her tumbling to the floor.

It was her cell.

Call the police, and he dies.

When a car shows up, you just stay put. It's your husband we need, not you.

Just back away, and go home. You'll be fine.

But if you try to get cute, you both die.

Helen's heart thumped loud enough for her to hear it. She stared at the factory, seeing no movement inside. Nothing.

"What's... going on?" McCoy asked, his eyes still on her but losing life.

Mouth and eyes wide open, Helen kept staring. She pulled her gaze away from the factory and checked her body, seeing a few cuts, shards of glass in her legs, and the gun laying there on the floor in the space behind the front seat. She swallowed hard and answered McCoy's question. "They have him. Just like you said. They won."

She scooped the gun from the floor and grasped it, testing to see if her hand was strong enough to grip it. It was.

Aiming it at the floor just as McCoy taught her, she opened the chamber, checking to make sure it was fully loaded. Then, she snapped it shut and pulled back the hammer.

"What… are you… doing?" He asked.

"I'm getting my husband back," she answered. The words seemed to catch her by surprise, as if said by somebody else. But as she stared at the factory, it didn't seem like there was any other way to get him back alive.

Helen charged out of the car, put off by the uneasy silence surrounding her. She raised the gun to her hip just like she saw McCoy do earlier. Her finger rested uncomfortably against the trigger guard, ready to shoot if needed, but praying she wouldn't have to.

Up close, the factory had an almost haunted feel to it. The walls had collected years of dust and graffiti. The windows were so coated with gunk that everything inside looked foggy and unfocused.

She leaned close to a window, seeing nothing or nobody unusual. A long, wooden floor stretched down a hallway that led to nothing but more walls and a series of steel tables covered with grime.

A glance in the other direction revealed something shocking. An armed man with a cellphone at his ear circled a body on the floor. The prone body lay there motionless, eyes open but lifeless. It was Rex. A gasp shot from Helen's throat.

"Please, God, please!" she said, bending at her waist, then snapping up again for another glance to make sure she was seeing what she thought she was seeing. She repeated her shaky words. "Please, God, please!"

The man above her husband moved in spastic jerks, fueled by nervous energy and perhaps regret. He screamed into the phone.

She leaned in closer, noticing what looked like a breathing motion from the supine body. Tears flooded her vision, but she stabbed them away and noticed his head jerk to the window. He saw her.

She pressed her hand flat against the window to let him know she was okay. For now.

His face eased into a grin, probably saying the same thing. He had to know the situation was dire, but, as always, he needed her to know he was there for her.

The man standing above Rex noticed nothing of the wordless conversation between husband and wife. He screamed into his phone; his words nearly audible from outside.

After a cautious glance around, Helen pressed her ear against the window, her head angled so it could remain hidden behind a cobweb. She held still to make sure she could hear every word shouted.

"I don't care if you need this guy alive!" the man barked. "If you don't get somebody out here to get me in three minutes, he's dead!" More circling around Rex, his gun shifting between his head and chest.

Helen pulled away to see if there was anything else important that she could see. But there was nothing else there. Just a long, empty hallway painted with dust and occupied with nothing but her husband and the man poised to kill him.

When the man screamed more, Helen pressed her ear against the window again to pick up the rest. "Listen to me! I do not care how much of a pain in the ass it is to get somebody out here, I—"

The man turned and froze, his eyes angrily aimed out the window. He sprang toward her, gun outstretched.

In the half-second before he reached the window, she weighed her options in slow-motion. She could shoot at the window, hoping to hit him. Or she could duck under the window.

Shooting would have been a better choice. It was a close shot, closer than the makeshift targets she shot at during target practice with McCoy. He was right there.

But whatever courage was needed to make the shot abandoned her in the half-second that followed. She ducked below the window, eyes slammed shut in wordless prayer.

A car passed by the factory on the dirty road several yards away. It occurred to Helen that the guy looked not at her, but at the car. That was what brought him to the window.

For five, maybe ten, seconds, she sat there without moving, hoping her hunch was right. She heard nothing for close to a minute, then footsteps raced away from the window.

A deep voice yelled "Nooo!" loud enough to be heard without her ear against the window. It was a voice she recognized. It was Rex.

Lifting her body back up, she saw the man above her husband, his gun aimed at his head. She had to do something. No other choice.

With her elbow, she smashed the window open, then aimed her gun through it.

The man's body had turned to her, his gun rising up but was not there yet. She squeezed the trigger, waited for that hard smack of metal.

The man's body jerked back as if electrocuted, his gun tumbling from his grip to the floor. He reached for it as Rex's face turned to her, mouth wide with shock.

Helen took a second shot at the man as he fumbled for his gun, but she guessed that she'd missed him.

When she took a third shot, he raced down the hallway, head ducked low to avoid any more bullets.

She crawled through the window, clumsily diving inside and reaching the floor with an echoed thud. "Rex!" she yelled. "We gotta get you out of here!"

She dropped to the floor to inspect his face. He breathed hard, his face creased in pain. "What the hell did you just do?" he yelled.

Through a breathless laugh, she said, "I did what I had to do to get you out of here. Now, let's go!"

But a glance at his paralyzed face made it clear that things wouldn't be that simple.

He buckled into a series of quakes, his lips tugged downward into a hard frown, his knees curling toward his chest. It was that look again. The one that put on horrific display the damage done to him in combat. It was a PTSD flashback.

She tried to shush him, caress his spastic body into a calmer, more settled state, but it was no use. It didn't work when the symptoms first appeared, and it didn't work now. There was nothing to do but wait it out. If there was time.

Helen jabbed a hand into her pocket, reaching for her cellphone—a call to 911 was her only hope—but wild swings of her husband's head slapped it out of her hand, sending it crashing to the floor. It landed in a lightning strike of a shatter.

Footfalls down the hallway came closer, picking up speed. She could hear the metallic clack of a gun and the grunts of a man eager to avenge a wound.

She looked at Rex's shaking body, assessing his weight as his sputtered yelps filled the hallway with echoes.

With her options racing away from her, she grabbed his

torso, sliding his body toward her. In a clunky motion, she tried to lift him over her shoulder, but this was going to be harder than she expected. Carrying him out of the factory wasn't an option.

The footsteps got closer, angrier.

Helen tried to grip the gun in her shaky hand, knowing she had to use it. She climbed to a crouched stance and faced the hallway.

It took a second or two for the man to see what had happened. First, he froze in place, then dropped to his knees.

Helen fired the gun, but her trembling hands sent the bullet sailing askew. It landed with a clank, perhaps hitting a wall or the floor or something else. She couldn't tell.

The guy leapt to his side, out of her view and sprang down another hallway.

She spun, trying to guess where her target was headed and why. Ignoring Rex's explosion of shudders wasn't easy. Just like she couldn't erase those barks that stabbed at her ear drums. But she had to focus, had to figure out her next move.

The footfalls disappeared. Wherever the guy was, he was a good distance away. Great news. She had time.

After giving the room a good scan, she spotted a pile of black boxes in the corner, probably not thick enough to provide cover, but at least it was a place to hide, a place to buy a second or two. Maybe. Hiding would clearly be a problem with Rex's noises.

She grabbed her husband's shoulders, fingernails digging deep in the fabric of his shirt, dragging him across the giant room just as footsteps came closer and closer.

They reached the boxes, and Helen slid Rex into place, cupping his mouth shut with shivering hands.

But it didn't help. If anything, it urged him into a greater sense of panic and louder screams. The plan wouldn't work. The guy was bound to enter the room and immediately discern their location. She needed a plan B.

As the footfalls crept closer, an idea hit her.

She'd leave behind the boxes, using him as a decoy while she set up to take a shot.

Glancing at his pained face brought tears to her eyes, regret already pouring into her body. "I'll be back, I promise," she whispered to him, touching his face.

Then, it was time to go.

In a crouch, she backed away from the hiding place, then slipped to their original location, the corner where the room met the hallway.

She made every effort to steady her gun hand, trying deep breaths, clenched teeth, strokes at her thighs. Nothing worked. She was scared to death, and there was no way to hide it, no way to eliminate it.

The guy sprinted into the room from the hallway opening just across from her. Rex's barks brought his eyes and gun barrel straight to the pile of boxes—just as she planned.

Helen knew she'd only have a second. So, she raced through the steps McCoy had taught her, lifting her gun in a fast-motion, tugging the trigger before giving herself a chance to truly consider what she was doing.

The gunshot shook her hands and wrists exactly as the guy turned, his eyes gigantic, his every tooth bared.

His body hit the ground before Helen could guess where she hit him. All she knew was that he was down. And not likely to get up anytime soon.

As she stood and took tiny steps closer, the room now had two deep voices sputtering out of control. But one of them slowly faded. By the time she reached him, he lay there, eyes fluttering shut, a dark red stain just below his shoulder. He tried to say something but barely had the vigor to push it through his lungs.

Helen backed away from the target and lunged for her husband, smothering him in a hug. Her hand thumped against something rigid in his breast pocket. A cellphone.

She pulled his phone out with one hand and kept him roped in a hug with the other, dialing frantically as his tears moistened her shoulder.

"911, what is your emergency?"

She collected her breath just enough to say a few words. "We need help."

By now, Rex's body had been quelled. Together, they managed a weak grin.

"We're going to be alright, honey," she told him. "We're going to be alright. I promise."

BEAR HUNT

Clayton Morrell was not a man who tossed things into his duffel and left in a hurry. He was precise, meticulous, and always prepared. The evening before he boarded his flight to Anchorage, where he would rendezvous with Slaterline, he double and triple checked his bag.

Everything that he packed was new, top-of-the-line, proven, and expensive. High-tech thermal base layers, goggles with polarized lenses that would not fog in extreme temperatures, and sub-zero gloves with a ready trigger finger; even his socks were something out of a lab where very smart people were paid to keep the ultra-rich ultra-comfortable while they exercised their exclusive pastimes.

In the corners of the duffel were traces of sand from the Gobi Desert leftover from last month's excursion. The bottom of the bag was scuffed from being dragged over boulders and through snags in the Amazon. There was a small rip in the side where he had caught it on a Whistling Thorn shrub in the African savanna.

Everywhere that Clayton traveled, he sought the biggest, most dangerous, or most elusive creatures, and he always brought all of them down. The walls of his lavish and expansive den were a testament to his prowess in the field, as heads of wild beasts, tigers and wolves, hung from every surface, each frozen forever in a vicious snarl meant to represent the beast within Clayton's own heart. A massive Great White shark hung from the rafters with blood-red paint dabbed on its side to show where Clayton had pierced the beast from the deck of a 30-foot schooner. The floors were covered in the broad and beautiful hides of a dozen rare animals, and the lamps were constructed from the legs of giraffes or mountain sheep. He had an ashtray made from the foot of an African elephant.

Clayton Morrell had to believe that his renown as a hunter was worldwide, because everywhere he went, he was greeted by throngs of protesters: the tree-hugging animal activist types who thought no creature should ever fall under the hand of a man, no matter how rich he was.

He suspected that this trip would be no different, though he harbored a small hope that, when he landed at the airport at 2 in the morning, the biting wind and razor sleet would be too unpleasant for any soft-hearted protesters with their cardboard signs and idealistic slogans.

Slaterline would be there to cover him if there were any lunatics willing to brave the weather, but it would be easiest if he could get to his hotel suite without any drama. He relished the night before a hunt since he shirked most creature comforts during the hunt itself. The night before he set off, he had made a habit of booking a suite at the best hotel the area had to offer, eating a fine meal at a luxurious pace and often entertaining the company of a beautiful woman—at least before turning her away and hitting the Egyptian cotton sheets for a night of uninterrupted rest.

He felt that the women helped to relieve him of any sympathy that might lurk in his veins, any flaw that may have caused him to hesitate before squeezing the trigger. Slaterline was in charge of arranging suitable dates for the eve of a hunt, and he always knew what Clayton liked.

Zipping the duffel closed, Clayton carried it to the hallway and set it out for the butler to load into the waiting car. He did not know the name of this particular butler— he hadn't bothered to learn it. They seldom lasted long enough to be worth knowing, and he did not doubt that this one would be gone long before the end of bear season.

Bear season was the reason why Clayton was willing to suffer an undesirable flight through frigid skies and the inhospitable weather of Alaska in early winter. Grizzlies could only be legally killed before the turn of the New Year, and Clayton, while perhaps morally ambivalent in the boardroom, was no common poacher. The hunt would mean missing

Christmas, but that was a plus for Clayton: he had no one with which he wished to share the holidays. He had never married, was not in contact with any of his illegitimate children, save for their monthly checks, and he had no desire to sit down and carve the Christmas ham with his senile and audacious mother. All the better that he spent the yuletide scaling rocky ledges and seeking the biggest and most dangerous mammals on the continent.

"No, not quite the most dangerous," he thought, catching sight of himself in the mirror. *"But a close second."*

He had traveled twice before to Alaska with the aim of adding a grizzly to his trophy room. The first time he had been fouled by the weather, as it had stormed for the entire week he was there, making it impossible to see, much less track, a bear. He would have stayed longer and waited out the weather, but news of his father's death came, and Clayton was dragged home by some lingering sense of propriety.

The second time he went in search of grizzlies, he had fallen ill on the first day of the hunt. His fever soared to frightening heights, and he swore that he could see massive bears every time he opened his eyes. He was finally sent home by his guides, who refused to take another step into the mountains with a wild-eyed man who continually pointed his rifle at them.

This time, he was certain of his success, and he was thrilled at the thought of taking down such a mighty animal. There was a spot reserved for the mount in his den and a taxidermist on standby. He had been self-quarantining, taking vitamins and supplements to ensure that mistake never happened again. And if his mother died while he was away, so be it; nothing was going to ruin this hunt for him.

Douglas Slaterline stood at the edge of the tarmac and

squinted against the wind and sleet. There was a distant light that he knew was the jet carrying Clayton Morrell and perhaps a handful of other wealthy souls, all converging on Alaska for their own sinful reasons. Five years of being Clayton's assistant/henchman had shown Slaterline another universe— a world that existed within and parallel to the normal one but would be forever invisible to most people in society.

The general population thought that the rich primarily vacationed in the typical hotspots: Vail for skiing, the Caribbean for sun, France or Italy when taste and culture were in order. The "ordinary" rich— the mere millionaires and hedge fund managers with their new money— truly did frequent these locales. The *ultra*-rich were content to let the world believe that those places represented the pinnacle of luxury. As long as the ordinary Dicks and Janes hoarded their pennies to fly to Rome for their fortieth wedding anniversary, to schmooze with who they thought were the rich and famous, then they wouldn't be invading the real paradises that the richest of the rich had carved out in hard-to-reach places all over the world.

Clayton Morrell was not necessarily one of the ultra-rich, but he was almost like their patron saint. Clayton went places that were rough and dangerous, hot or cold, or altogether unwelcoming. He spared no expense in taking his treks and in bringing back his trophies. Over the years, others followed in his footsteps, but instead of bringing guns and camo, they came with money and architects. Slaterline knew how much Clayton resented seeing his remote escapes become dotted with micro-mansions and three-story log cabins, but the esteem that he received from being the designated trailblazer for the one-percent was enough to soothe his irritation. He was more than a celebrity in the wilds of rich society: he was their idol.

The jet touched down and roared across the runway, sending up a spray of white mist and scattering a dozen sea birds in a screeching and chattering cacophony. It had scarcely powered down its engines before darkly-clad passengers began to disembark. They were not the esteemed visitors to the vast and frigid north; these were their servants and assistants, highly paid and highly trained lackeys to procure luggage, safety deposit boxes, treasured pets. Behind them came the precious human cargo: individuals with unimaginable wealth and names that very few were familiar with. Old money moguls and secret royalty, those who whispered into the ears of the most powerful people in the world— the true decision makers of the age.

They didn't look like much, Slaterline thought. He failed to be impressed by their finery, their gait and posture. They all seemed frail to him, even the relatively young ones. Perhaps this was because Slaterline was accustomed to watching this parade play out exactly as it did now: the servants, then the highest of high society, and finally, at the end, Clayton Morrell would emerge from his seat at the back of the jet.

Clayton shared nothing in his appearance with his fellow passengers. Not his manner of dress, not his luggage, not his demeanor. Those who were almost his peers stepped onto the tarmac in tailored Armani suits and designer lounge wear, all draped with goose down parkas and overcoats that cost more than brand new cars— though not any car that these people would be seen in. Clayton, by contrast, emerged in jeans and boots, his thick flannel buttoned not quite to the neck. He wore no coat or hat, for this was not to be the truly cold part of his adventure, and his thick, dark hair was tousled by the winds.

The other passengers were withdrawn, vapid, deferring to their assistants and bodyguards as though they were of an altogether separate form of life, only acknowledging them when they had a need. Clayton scanned the tarmac immediately, seeking out Slaterline. When he saw him, he gave him a wide and confident smile. As always, Slaterline reached for Clayton's carry-on bag, and as always, Clayton refused to let him have it.

"You know I'm quite capable, Slat, of carrying my own weight."

"I sure do, sir, but you ain't paying me to stand here shivering."

"Shivering? Who's cold?" Clayton replied with a hearty chuckle. "We're not even at the good part yet."

While the others headed to their four-wheel-drive limos and left their staff to collect their many suitcases, Clayton and Slaterline each shouldered the few bags of gear that had been stowed in the belly of the jet. This would be the first time that Slaterline touched the gear for this trip, but he knew from experience that nothing would have been forgotten, not a bullet or sock left behind. His employer was nothing if not conscientious about his hunts.

"How's the room, Slat? Up to snuff?"

"Definitely, boss," Slaterline replied, referring to the sprawling suite that he had reserved for Clayton, a luxurious space that was fully stocked with food and drink and boasted a wide fireplace and a deep bed.

"But you've received an invitation from the Duchess. She's throwing some kind of party tonight."

Clayton looked momentarily annoyed, and he turned to scan the terminal for the Duchess, who was no real Duchess by monarchistic standards, but who undoubtedly owned more, knew more, and controlled more than any "real" Duchess of the modern era.

He was about to send Slaterline to politely refuse her offer — he had certain rituals which he liked to attend to on the night before a hunt— but when he spotted her leaving the terminal with all of her three daughters in tow, his expression changed from annoyed to intrigued.

The Duchess's daughters were all in their twenties, and each could have been a model for any magazine in the world—had they any need for money or employment at all. Indeed, to be featured in even the glossiest of periodicals would have been far beneath the station of these three girls. There were levels of prestige in this world that looked down at even celebrities with disdain.

"Well, buddy," Clayton said. "Better put a shine on your best boots. Looks like we're going to a ball."

****

Later that night, as Clayton Morrell left a lavish party with a young heiress on his arm, a man whom he had never met carefully navigated the mountain slopes, the knobby tires of his old Jeep gripping the snow and slush as he made his way around switchback after switchback.

The man had been at the airport when Morrell's jet arrived. He, too, had been thankful for the lack of protesters and picketers. He was forever annoyed by these impotent shriekers with their signs and empty threats. All they ever did was talk, but when the powers-that-be rolled in, they all shrank like flowers in the frost. It didn't matter if it was oil barons or prospectors or big game hunters, the soft-skinned idealists in Anchorage let them all through their lines with hardly more than a shout.

No. Shame would never stop these people. And there was not enough money in all of Alaska to buy them off. As the Jeep labored its way into higher and higher altitudes, the man looked down at the lights of the capitol city and thought of the one thing that might actually put a stop to all of the destruction he had witnessed in his life.

Fear.

Fear was a language that anyone could understand. Rich or poor, old or young, everyone could feel fear. If people refused to listen to reason, turned their backs on earnest pleas and calls for civility, then he would wield fear as a weapon.

He had watched Morrell and his hired man reunite—had been watching Slaterline since he arrived. He knew where Morrell would lay his head that night and what trail he would take up the mountain in the morning. The man shook his head and admonished himself for having false hopes. He had hoped that Morrell might drink too much tonight, miss his rendezvous with the guides in the morning. Or better yet, that his hangover would be enough to send him stumbling off a mountain pass. But anyone who knew anything about Clayton Morrell knew that he put his passion ahead of his lust, and that he would be up long before the crack of dawn, ready to scale whatever cliffs necessary in order to stalk his magnificent prey.

No. It would not be that easy. But he was prepared, had been readying himself for this moment for months. The great, white, spoiled hunter was bound to come soon enough, and he had made his preparations.

Yes, Rodney Combs was ready to protect his friends, his land, his convictions. The bears were his brethren, the land was his church. Clayton Morrell was a demon on borrowed time.

After a while, he took a turn away from the sheer cliffs and the astounding views of the city. He drove inland and ever upwards, the sky clearing as he passed the storm line. He was greeted by brilliant stars in a sea of obsidian, the road finally leveling out as he approached his humble cabin.

The dog waiting in the yard barked, glad to see its owner coming home. There were no lights on in the house and would not be until he flipped the switch for the solar batteries. Cold turnips and potatoes waited to be cooked in the cast iron skillet. His meals came from the earth; they never walked upon it.

Inside, iron contraptions with sharp teeth and sturdy chains scattered across his dining room table. His traps were laid out, oiled and checked over. It had been many years since he had laid a trap line— a man who ate only plants had little use for snares and iron jaws— but there had been a time, years ago, when some arrogant trespassers had necessitated the need for such measures. Their blood still stained some of the traps, and he left it alone in reverence of the hunt and in memory of his victory. Clayton Morrell was not the only man on the mountain who took pride in his quarry. Still, there was no season for disrespectful men; they had to be hunted illicitly and disposed of with great care.

The dog lay beneath the table and gnawed on a bone of dubious origin. Outside the cold, still air would soon be filled with the huffing and groaning of many lumbering bears. They would be hungry, but he would not feed them at this time. There was a meal to be had, but it slept in the city, wrapped in silk and sin, a wealthy woman against his greedy chest.

Rodney hummed and bent to his whetstone as his dinner cooked on the fire. The sound of his knife against the stone mingled with the hungry tones of the bears outside his home, making a strange symphony that he imagined might be the score to a drama, a scene that had yet to unfold.

The traps, the bears, the knife. All sharp things that would defend the land and the precious souls who lived upon it. There was not enough monetary value in ten square miles to begin to equal what Clayton Morrell wasted in a day. He thought he could buy the rights to any soul he desired, to destroy it and take the empty husk home with him. Rodney had seen the magazines about Morrell's home, his debauched decorations. He could not reach out and rescue the zebras and jaguars, the antelope and moose who had already been slaughtered. But he could certainly protect his friends from this man, this monster. It had been done before, and it would be done again. A rich man died as easily as a poor one. The rules of mortality cared nothing for a man's net worth.

In the city below, Clayton Morrell did indeed lay in a soft bed with the tawny head of a beautiful woman on his chest, but sleep would not come for him. Clayton's mind was whirring with anticipation, calculations, checklists and scenarios. He cursed himself. He should have drunk a little more, or at least not brought home the Duchess's daughter. He felt over-stimulated and wound up. He would sleep poorly, if at all, and that was a bad way to begin a hunt.

There had been no picketers or protesters at the airport, and that was lucky, but there had been the one man, the one in the green army coat that Clayton had glanced at on his way to the Hummer. The man's inactivity was the only reason he had noticed him. In an airport full of busy and important people, he was the only body holding still— and he was looking directly at Clayton.

The stranger looked to be about the same age as Clayton, and he had close-cropped dark hair, just turning white at the edges. He wore a full beard and a scowl, but what was most disconcerting was his eyes. There was a heat in his stare, a calculated and contained vehemence, something that managed to reach across the wide airport terminal and touch Clayton like a branding iron.

Clayton knew he should have approached the man and introduced himself, extended a hand, maybe greased the man's palm. But there was just something about the man's countenance that warned him off. And now, as he laid between the sheets and waited for sleep, that face, those furious eyes, kept playing across the screen of his imagination.

****

"Get the rest of your shit loaded, and let's get moving!" Slaterline shouted over the wind. He was looking at the screen he held in his hand. It showed a mass of green and yellow moving across a map of the countryside, a menacing spot of red at its center.

"This storm isn't going to wait on us. We're gonna get up that mountain before the worst of it hits. Then, we can hunker down until it clears."

He was not shouting at Clayton. His employer already sat in the front passenger seat of the lead Hummer, had been there since before half of the guides even pulled into the parking lot. The recipients of Slaterline's barked orders were the three fully-fledged guides and three of their apprentices that milled around the two black Hummers, looking for empty space to stash their gear, guns, and provisions.

The established plan had outlined a 6 a.m. departure time, leaving adequate time to get up the mountain, set up a base camp, and do some scouting before nightfall. But a storm had rolled in, and in these parts, storms moved fast. Slaterline had been up since 3:30, calling guides and rousing them from their warm beds. They would be leaving ASAP, or preferably sooner, was what he told each man when they answered the phone with groggy voices.

It was now 5:15, and Slaterline cursed as he watched the satellite images on his notebook.

"We're rolling out now!" he shouted. "If your ass isn't in a seat in twenty seconds, you're walking up that mountain."

Doors slammed, engines roared, and eight knobby snow tires spun, found traction, and spit plumes of snow mixed with the roiling exhaust and was dispelled to the morning darkness by winds that seemed to grow stronger by the minute. Slaterline rode in the lead vehicle, sitting directly behind Clayton. The driver was a local guide named Diggy Palmer. He looked to be about fifty years old and had a gray beard down to his belt buckle and a mischievous smile on his face.

"Better git to gittin'," Palmer said. "Or we'll be snowed in and picking our teeth at the Anchorage Bar and Grill until spring."

"Gittin' is your job," Slaterline grunted from the back seat. "Put the pedal down, and if those other guys don't keep up, you'll get their share at the end of the hunt."

Palmer grinned and gunned the engine. The Hummer growled and fishtailed wildly as he took an exit, and they left the lights of Anchorage behind, barreling headlong toward the distant mountains, invisible in the dark and snow but somehow emitted a force, an energy that could be felt from far away.

The other vehicle did not fall behind, and the micro caravan wound its way through scrubby brush lands and low hills until they began to climb, causing everyone's ears to pop. Slaterline chewed gum in the back seat and handed a stick up to his boss, who accepted it without a word. Clayton was not looking at the snow that flashed past in the glare from the headlights or at the mountain peaks that slowly began to appear as though in a shadow box, the dim light of a stormy morning marking the sky a dull gray.

Clayton was absorbed in a notebook, a journal the he carried with him on every hunt. He was using the dim light from the dashboard to write. Slaterline knew that he would record every detail of the hunt, even this boring ride, even the way that Slaterline handled the guides. Clayton would draw pictures in the margins, sketches of ridgelines or trees, paw prints, hoof prints, the eyes of his fallen prey.

There was more than a dozen of these leather-bound notebooks on a shelf in Clayton's study, and he took one down from time to time to study and remember his successes as well as his failures. This drive to commit everything to memory was a part of Clayton's life strategy. He relied on no one to tell him what was true, and he was suspicious of nearly everyone. Everyone besides Slaterline.

They had met in a bar of all places. It had been more than a decade prior, and the two had found themselves drinking at a lodge in southern Utah. Slaterline was guiding a group of middle-class hacks on a hunt for chukar partridges and sage grouses. Clayton had flown in to shoot the biggest antelope he could find. Both had been successful enough that they were sufficiently lubricated with scotch and bourbon by the time they struck up a conversation.

Clayton, who at that point was relatively unheard of in big game circles, already had guides in every corner of the planet. He was not at a loss for professional assistance when it came to his hunting, but there was something more specific and nefarious that he was looking for in a hired man. He noticed the tattoos on Slaterline's hands and arms, the two tiny daggers inked on the side of his neck, and he went ahead and asked the question that he needed answered.

"Well, yes," Slaterline told him. "I've served time, plenty enough of it. I've gone straight now, though."

Clayton had smiled with pleasure, leaned back, and polished off his glass of scotch.

"I hope that's not entirely true," he said.

The rest was history. Clayton wanted a man who would

do whatever was necessary— legal barricades be damned— to help him get to the places he needed to go to kill the species he wanted to kill. Slaterline had initially been reluctant to once more go outside of the law, but the cash came in thick envelopes every month, and soon, his conscience was assuaged.

Now, Clayton closed his notebook and rubbed his eyes. He looked tired. Slaterline wondered how late the Duchess's girl had kept him up, but he knew better than to ask about things like that. Their relationship was amiable, could even be called a friendship, but there were things that were none of his business.

"How, how long until we reach the site?" Clayton asked.

"About another hour," Palmer said. "Still time to get a little extra shuteye, if that suits you."

Clayton shook his head and watched the gray world go by outside the Hummer's windows. He was unlikely to sleep more than a couple of hours a night for the duration of the hunt. Slaterline was equipped with all manner of uppers and amphetamines that he could administer to his boss at a moment's notice, should the big man decide he was in need of a pick-me-up. Sleep was not what he came here for.

Another half an hour passed in silence, the only sound the growl of the Hummer and the occasional whistle or hum from Palmer, who did not seem accustomed to such stoic passengers. Slaterline was surprised that the guide never reached for the radio dial. If he had, Clayton would have slapped his hand away. Slaterline had seen him do it before. On the way back down the mountain, Clayton himself might crank up some Creedence Clearwater Revival or Ted Nugent, may even sing along. But on the way to camp, he was interested in nothing but the company of his own meticulous thoughts.

They had stopped climbing and now rounded a wide turn, a sheer rock face on one side and a harrowing drop-off on the other. Palmer's knuckles were white on the steering wheel. All at once, the vehicle seemed to lunge toward the rock wall, and there was a terrific banging sound. Slaterline knew they had blown a tire even before the front corner of the Hummer crashed against the rock and the rear end spun around. Palmer cursed violently and wrestled with the wheel, trying to correct the skid. They spun completely backward and finally came to a precarious stop, the rear tires of the vehicle only inches from the edge of the cliff.

The second Hummer came crawling up in low gear, stopping with its headlights in their eyes. Slaterline climbed out of the back seat and shouted for the others to cut the lights. Once everyone was out and Palmer's heart had resumed a normal rhythm, they inspected the damage. The left front tire was a shredded mess of rubber, the driver's side headlight was gone, and the radiator was damaged.

Slaterline examined the obliterated tire with a cold feeling in his gut. He walked back down the snowy trail in the direction they had come from. It was scarcely more than a two-track at this point, and the footing was slippery, the wind cruel. About thirty paces down the road, he found what he had hoped he would not. A jagged maw of blackened steel protruded from the fresh powder, its teeth sharp and firmly clenched.

Another guide approached, carrying a trekking pole, and stared down at the bear trap without a word. Slaterline took the pole from the man's hand and began to prod around in the surrounding snow with it, stepping only in places that he had already probed.

Snap.

Another trip exploded from the drift, slamming closed with a terrible metallic sound.

Snap.

A third sounded with a resounding shudder. Slaterline kept looking for a few more minutes but found no other traps in the road. He carried the first trap back to where the Hummers sat idle.

"Looks like someone isn't too happy about us being on the mountain," he said, dropping the trap at Palmer's feet.

Clayton studied the device with detached calm, though a vein in his neck danced in a menacing way.

"Palmer," Clayton said. "You're from these parts. Do you have any idea who might be willing to put my life at risk to keep us off this hunt?"

Palmer was still staring at the bear trap, his hands buried deep in the pockets of his parka. He stood that way for a long time before deciding on how to answer.

"Mr. Morrell," he finally said, not meeting Clayton's eyes. "People all over the world know who you are and what you do. I don't have to tell you that you've got what you might call…some detractors. But I would be remiss in my duties as your guide right now if I didn't level with you."

He finally raised his eyes to meet Clayton's stony gaze.

"This here is Alaska. This is where people go when they can't live anywhere else without getting thrown in jail or some other kind of trouble. Mister, if you've got an enemy here, you've got an enemy for life."

****

The second Hummer was suddenly very crowded.

The storm continued to whip its way through the pass,

and time was short. Clayton refused to send the working vehicle back for a wrecker, said that waiting for a replacement was out of the question. They would stay ahead of the storm in the second Hummer, and they could deal with the consequences later.

Eight men piled into one vehicle, Palmer acquiesced to let another guide drive, and they continued the slow voyage across the icy pass.

"A bear trap road block," Clayton said. "What kind of insane rednecks do you have up here, anyway?"

He had directed the question at no one in particular, but one of the guides in the back answered: "The bad kind."

They trundled along, every man waiting for another wreck, another flat, the other shoe to fall. But nothing happened, and before the sun was more than a bleary orb in the eastern clouds, they pulled into the flat and somber wasteland that would be their home for the next several days.

The spot was chosen because it was moderately sheltered from the wind. There was a moderate cliff along the western edge, which helped to block the gales, and a brambly patch of pines walled in the north and east. It was only to the south that the clearing was open, and the view across that desolate expanse was enough to take away a man's breath and strike fear in his heart, all at once.

The land rose and fell like waves on a tumultuous sea, black sheets of rock teetered and broken over the eons and snarls of spruce and cedar growing in tiny deposits of soil between boulders. It just went on and on until it reached a white and distant wall, the sheer ascent to the next peak, which was a towering monolith that greatly resembled a fang and pointed up into the sky as though to challenge God in heaven.

"Put the mess tent over by those trees," Slaterline ordered as the men began to unpack the gear that had been lashed to the top of their remaining transport. "Mr. Morrell's lodging will go by the foot of the cliff, with mine beside it. Someone start gathering wood for a fire. Be careful with those gas canisters, we only have enough for the week."

The storm continued to rage in the sky above, but the environment in the flat, covered area was much more hospitable. Slaterline found and scouted out the spot using a GPS feed that was intended for the U.S. military— Clayton Morrell's connections ran deep, and there was no underestimating the value of a well-placed bribe. Slaterline looked around at the site, seeing it for the first time in person, and was pleased with the setup. By mid-afternoon, they would be fully operational, and he knew that Clayton would insist that they go out and scout for signs of a grizzly. Slaterline was confident they would find plenty: this part of the mountain was crawling with the huge beasts. He had confirmed that fact and confirmed it again, checking with every guide and hunter in the state. This had to be the trip when Clayton finally slayed a monster— Slaterline had no desire to travel to Alaska again. He had plans on retiring to Hawaii before he was too old to enjoy the beaches.

Clayton's huge lodge tent was fully setup, and Slaterline's was nearly there as well. The two men stood by the Hummer and supervised as the men carried more gear into the temporary dwellings. Portable gas stoves, cots, lanterns, and waterproof bags of clothing.

Clayton was getting impatient. Impatient enough that he bent to help a smallish guide carry the big gas stove into his tent. Slaterline motioned angrily for one of the other men to take over for the boss. He wasn't paying this kind of money to put his back out hauling his own stove around in the snow.

Another man came and relieved Clayton, who came back

to stand next to Slaterline and watched as the two hired men disappeared into the big tent with the heater.

"You found a good spot to call home," Clayton said. "I could just about move in full time."

Slaterline scoffed. "Give it a couple years. Some of your pals from New York or Cali will have built a chalet right here. There'll be a helicopter pad right over there."

Clayton might have laughed at the joke, but the sound was lost in a crushing, crashing sound, something from above that was loud enough to be heard over the wind of the passing storm. Slaterline looked up just in time to see a boulder the size of a golf cart come smashing down the incline and land directly in the middle of Clayton's tent.

The yellow canvas billowed out like a skirt as the tent collapsed in a burst of snow and dust. Men were shouting, running in all directions and swearing, but no sound came from within the flattened tent.

Slaterline looked up to the edge of the cliff and blinked. He could swear he saw someone looking down at them, but then, the apparition was gone.

"Up there!" he shouted, pointing. "I want two men up there, armed! Now!"

There was some dispute about who would be the two to climb to the top of the rise, but the remaining guides hashed it out pretty quickly once Slaterline racked a round into his rifle and gave them a look that he hadn't had to use since prison.

It didn't matter much who went, he decided. He probably knew what they would find. There would be some sort of a lever, probably a thick tree branch, maybe a heavy metal pipe. No one could move a rock like that without a little help from good old Archimedes.

He doubted, however, that they would find any prints clear enough to track. The winds were high, the powder light. Whoever it was that wanted Clayton Morrell dead was no fool.

****

Safely back in his cabin, Rodney Combs shut the door against the wind and snow and sat down to unstrap his snowshoes. The hound sniffed at his ankles and wagged its tail, thumping it against the table leg, the cold stove, a chair.

Combs was cursing under his breath as the ice melted from his mustache and dribbled down his chin, where it dripped off onto his brown coveralls. He knew it had been too good to be true. When he first discovered— through the outfitter grapevine —the location of Clayton's would-be basecamp, he had set about devising various traps and pitfalls for the coming hunter.

The bear traps on the trail were basic, likely to do little more than slow them down, but he thought he might get lucky and send a vehicle over the ridge and crashing into the tops of the pines so very far below. The boulder, however, had been an experiment in luck. He couldn't know just where Clayton would have his personal tent set up, but Combs took a guess and, with great effort and no small amount of ingenuity, had levered the rock into place above the spot where he himself would have pitched his tent, were he trying to set up camp in that place.

That morning, through his binoculars, Combs watched Clayton help a man struggling to take a gas stove into the tent. It couldn't be that easy, and Comb's knew that patience was the essence of the hunt, but he let his excitement get the better of him. To have the opportunity to eliminate Clayton Morrell before he had a chance to fire a single shot? How could he pass that up?

He had scrambled to his station and levered the boulder down into the clearing, then crouched down to watch the outcome of his hard work. What a splendid crash it made. And what incredible chaos it immediately caused below. But in all of the confusion, he raised his binoculars again to survey the scene and was crestfallen to see Clayton standing clear of the wreckage.

Combs groaned and hung the snowshoes on the wall, then bent to stoke his fire while he spoke to the dog.

"I got cocky, you know, old girl?"

The dog wagged her tail some more, tilted her head, and raised one ear.

"I shoulda known that rich prick wouldn't be packing in his own gear. Now, I've tipped my hand. They're all gonna be on high alert, and it's just gonna make this all that much more complicated."

The dog whined and pawed at its owner's pant leg.

"Oh, don't worry. They can't track me, not in this storm," he said. "But best keep your ears pricked in case they stumble across this place later on."

He sat down in a stuffed chair that was overlaid and heaped with blankets and afghans. He took a battered sheaf of papers from a drawer by the chair and held them up to the meager light that came in through the small windows.

"I've got plenty more in store, old girl," he said, absently. "There's more than rocks and traps that can kill you in these mountains."

Beneath the floorboards of the old cabin, something breathed heavily, snoring in its slumber. It clutched a large bone under its massive brown paw, long claws curling into the dirt.

The dog could hear it, smell it, knew its presence well. They had been raised together, still played together even.

Combs could not hear or smell the bear, but he knew it was there, resting deeply in the dark of the cellar. It was the reason— one of the many reasons— that he had made such preparations. Not all family was blood, but all family was worth shedding blood over.

Diggy Palmer was scared, and he did not scare easily.

Half a day in, and this trip was already snakebit. He'd nearly driven his Hummer off the edge of a cliff because some yahoo booby trapped the pass with bear traps, and now two of his best buddies were dead— mashed up like cat food— before camp was even set up.

To make matters worse, the valley they had traveled into was a dead zone— they were out of radio range.

"We gotta head back and get ahold of the sheriff, DNR, somebody," he was telling Clayton and Slaterline. "They'll get a chopper up here and start searching for this lunatic, and we can be far away when it happens."

Neither man said anything for a time. They were in Palmer's tent, which was a bit crowded for the three large men but had been commandeered by Clayton nonetheless, considering the condition of his own lodging.

Slaterline looked toward the sky, a hard but calm look on his face.

"Not in this weather," he said. "No helicopter is going up until this storm clears. No point."

"That's right," Clayton agreed. "And it's too dangerous to turn back. They safest thing to do is to proceed as planned."

"Proceed as planned?!" Palmer practically shrieked. "How can we proceed as planned when we've lost one Hummer and two guides to some remarkably *unplanned* circumstances? You mean to tell me that you wanna go ahead and stalk *bear* right now, even while *we* are being stalked by some yokel that probably hasn't come down off this mountain in twenty years?"

Clayton wrote in one of his notebooks and said nothing. Slaterline waited a moment and then replied dryly.

"Ain't been no twenty years," he said. "I saw a little cabin on the satellite imaging. Guy's got solar panels. He's no hermit, not completely at least."

Palmer looked back and forth from Slaterline to Clayton.

"Did you know about this?" he asked Clayton.

Clayton finished writing something and answered without looking up.

"If Slat thought it was something I needed to know, he would have told me. He does not waste my time with trivial information."

"Well, it seems to me that this information has now become fundamentally *un*-trivial!" Palmer shouted. "And if you knew where this place is, then why didn't you say so? Why not send a couple of guys there to take the sucker down?"

"Because". Slaterline said. "If I had done that, they would be dead by now. This guy is a survivalist. He would have traps set all around his property, and if they got through that, he could probably snipe them at a hundred paces. So, why don't you just sit tight and do what you're being paid to do?"

Palmer started to say something but checked himself. Slaterline had a point. He certainly didn't relish the thought of going after a killer, in this storm or any other kind of terrain.

"And speaking of pay," Clayton spoke up. "If my figures are correct, your potential salary has increased by twenty five percent, considering our recent rate of turnover regarding this venture."

Clayton's callousness was disgusting, but Palmer could do the math, and he was upside-down in his mortgage. Maybe if he lived through this hunt, he could keep from losing everything. Maybe Martha would even come back.

****

In time, the wind died down enough that the party was able to move about and finish setting up the camp. By early evening, Clayton was ready to go out scouting for signs. Diggy and one other guide came along, fully armed and watching the horizons, the cliffs, and the tree line. One walked ahead, the other behind. Clayton and Slaterline kept their eyes to the ground.

"Slat, you know I trust you; you've never given me any reason not to," Clayton said.

"Mmhmm."

"I have to ask you, though, why didn't you say anything about that cabin earlier? Seems like you would have thought about it after we found the traps in the road."

"I did."

"So, why didn't you say something?"

Slaterline looked up and scanned the terrain. His breath hung in the air in front of his face like smoke.

"Well," he began. "I guess you could say that I'm

embarrassed. I saw that cabin on the imaging, I knew what it was, but I didn't take into account the possible fallout."

Clayton shrugged, paused to examine a partial print in the snow. Looked like a wolf.

"Why would you? There are people living in all corners of this world. Mountains, deserts, swamps. You had no reason to suspect that this guy was going to be a problem."

Slaterline sighed. He pulled off one glove and dug into his pocket for a pack of cigarettes and a lighter. Lit one.

"Still," he said. "I let you down. It's my job to plan for problems like this. That's part of why I didn't want the other guys going after him. I want to do it myself."

He could see that Clayton raised his eyebrows, because the brown arches appeared over his polarized glasses.

"By yourself?"

"Yes."

"When?"

Slaterline took another drag and looked to the west. The sun was descending beyond a distant range. Day ended early in the valley. They needed to be getting back to camp soon.

"Nightfall," he said.

It was late in the evening, and the small fires that the men kept were guttering and fading as each man headed to their tents for the night. Palmer had to double up with one of the grunts, as Clayton was sleeping in his tent.

The men went to bed with their guns loaded and nearby. This was not odd for a hunting party in these parts— wolves alone posed enough of a threat that it would be foolish to sleep unarmed. But on this night, it was not wolves that caused the men to sleep fitfully or to jump at any sound. There was a greater danger in the cold and dark wilderness. Slaterline geared up and prepared to go out into the night in search of that threat.

The storm had taken a break for the night, and the stiff winds pushed the clouds eastward until a low, full moon could be seen just above the mountaintop. Stars began to blink into existence, and in the half-light, Slaterline checked and re-checked his ammunition, his gun, his GPS.

"So, this is it, here?" Clayton asked, pointing to a small, dark box on a satellite printout.

They were in Slaterline's tent. Clayton was examining the images as Slaterline finished preparations.

"Yeah, that's it. Only dwelling on this slope of the mountain, from what I can tell, and it's gotta be the home of some homicidal quack."

He checked his rifle, made sure his cartridge extensions were full, ensured that there was a round ready in the chamber, and wiped the lenses on his scope with a microfiber cloth. He also carried a sidearm: a nine-millimeter pistol that was loaded with hollow tips. At his waist was a broad hunting knife, sharpened to a razor's edge. He was clad head-to-toe in white, save for the yellow night-lenses of his polarized goggles.

Slaterline looked for all the world like he was going out for a hunt. And, in fact, he was.

In a higher place, across a switchback and beyond a frozen stream, there was a blind. It would have been called a hunting blind, because for all intents and purposes, that was what it was. But Combs did not consider himself a hunter, in most circumstances.

Yet, here he was, crouched in the dark and the shelter of this wooden box, nestled carefully between the trunks of massive conifers, silent and invisible in the night. He was not going to sit at home and wait for his enemies to come find him; he would hide on the wayside, watch with vigilance until they approached, and then, he would handle things his own way.

The moon illuminated the forest around him, giving him a clear and far sight into the wilds. The snow was unblemished, clean and smooth. No one had been this way in some time. His cabin was down the way, beyond the next rise and tucked next to the river in a stand of cedar. There, his dog was waiting, probably anxiously. Beneath the cabin, nothing slept. It was nighttime, and there was danger afoot. Everyone knew it. Every living thing on the mountain understood survival.

He heard it before he saw it, a faint whooshing sound, interspersed with the tiniest metallic clinking. The meter was right, and soon, Combs's eyes confirmed that he was correct, that he *had* heard the stride of a man coming across the virgin snow. Combs did not have night vision goggles, didn't need them to know that this was one of the men from the hunting camp. The dark silhouette lumbered quickly, the narrow barrel of a gun jutting above his head. The man would pass thirty yards below the blind.

The shape hung close to the edge of the wood. *Smart*, thought Combs, this was a man accustomed to stalking, and, perhaps, to being stalked. A worthy adversary, but he could tell it was not Clayton. This man was shorter and stockier, and Combs also guessed that Clayton would not hunt him on his own.

He lowered the plexiglass window of the blind soundlessly, holding his breath and watching to see if the man heard anything. He continued onward, and Combs bent to pick up his crossbow. Gunshots on a night like this would alert everyone back at the camp, and when their man did not return, they would know he was a goner and might come up in full force. The crossbow was a subtler option. At the very least, it could buy Combs a little more time.

There was already a bolt in the cradle, and Combs drew back and clicked the bowstring home. At that tiny sound, the man froze in his tracks. He looked like a deer that had heard a potential predator in the thicket, his ears practically standing up. Combs did not breathe.

Finally, after several agonizing seconds, the man began to slowly creep forward. His back was half to Combs now, as he was heading away, directly toward the cabin. Combs sighted on the middle of his back and let it fly with the crossbow. But in the instant that he pulled the trigger, the man dropped to the ground, rolled as the bolt whistled over his head, and fired a shot with a pistol that splintered the boards of the blind, right next to where Combs was perched.

So much for stealth, he thought.

Combs ducked before a second shot was fired, scrambled out the door at the back of the blind as splinters rained from above and caught in his hair and beard. He was out into the wild, white night in an instant, setting another bolt to shoot, running while bent low at the waist, his senses heightened by danger and adrenaline.

Combs ran in a wide semi-circle, slipped through a grove of fir trees that hung their branches low to the ground and provided excellent cover. When he stepped out from behind a rock face at the end of the grove, he sighted down on the spot where the man had been shooting from, but there was no one there. He looked in every direction, feeling suddenly exposed. The moon was high and bright.

There was nothing, only clear and frantic tracks leading

directly toward his home.

Slaterline had acted on instinct more than anything else. He'd had a feeling, and it was the same feeling that had saved his life in prison on more than one occasion.

He knew that his wild shot had been errant, had not expected to wound the man, but he also knew that he only had a matter of time and was not likely to get so lucky the next time around. This man knew the lay of the land, probably could navigate these woods with his eyes closed. Slaterline was at a disadvantage.

So, he made a snap decision to head for the cabin. There, he might be able to turn the tables, to obtain some kind of higher ground where he could see his adversary coming and take his time making a good, clean shot.

He knew that the cabin had to be just aways up ahead since he had studied the GPS map carefully before he left camp. If he could be the first one there, he might barricade himself inside and pick off his opponent when the time was right.

Slaterline could hear nothing in the frigid night but his own breathing, footfalls and perhaps the slamming rhythm of his own heart. He kicked up rooster tails of snow with each running step, eyes scanning the moonlit landscape in search of the cabin.

When he finally found it, he almost missed it. The dwelling sat in a low and shadowed space, next to a river that burbled softly. Snow had blanketed the roof and blown over the porch, rendering the place almost invisible in the moonlight.

He approached with practiced caution and tried the door. It was open. There could be more boobytraps, but if the man had rigged the house, he probably wouldn't have taken a potshot at Slaterline on his way there. He would have just let the traps do the work.

So, he slipped inside and closed the door silently behind him. He did not dare to even feel around for a light switch, though he knew that if there were solar panels, there must have been lights. There was no point in hiding; he hadn't had the time to cover his tracks. When the occupant returned, they would know he was inside. Something bumped his leg, and he spun and looked down. A medium-sized hound was sniffing his leg and wagging its tail. No threat there, but maybe something useful. He needed a plan.

Knowing that he probably didn't have much time, he searched about quickly in the dark. In the dim light from the narrow window, he examined the assorted items on what seemed to be a workbench. Arrow tips, spent shotgun shells, bits of stone or bone, hard to tell which in the dark.

There.

Slaterline seized upon a small role of fine wire, likely something that the lunatic used for making traps and trip lines. Wasting no time, he slipped back out of the door and set to work.

Combs approached the cabin with great care, biding his time. The place was dark, but this was certainly where his quarry had run off to. He would not be foolish enough to start turning on lights.

And then, he did.

Combs could hardly believe it, but he watched as a light turned on in his home. The white-clad man was in there, clearly visible. He had taken off his goggles and was crouched down in the middle of the floor. Combs moved through the trees, crossbow half-raised, trying to get a better angle on what the man was doing.

He froze, anger and disgust rising in his stomach and making his blood boil. Combs emitted a guttural snarl as he charged headlong toward the cabin. The man inside was kneeling on his dog, a knife to the poor hound's furry neck.

Combs rushed down the slope and across the small clearing to the porch steps. He would kick the door open and fire a bolt, hopefully puncturing the stranger's cranium before he could do anything more to hurt his poor dog. That dog was as innocent as any other creature in the wild. It was men who brought terror and evil and unnecessary death into the world.

With that last thought, Combs bounded onto his own front porch and had his head nearly removed from his body. Something that seemed both cold and hot sliced through his face, from the side of his chin up across his eye. He fell back and felt the pain sear his forehead and the front of his scalp.

Combs laid on his back on the porch boards, looking up through his one good eye at the thin slab of flesh that hung from a taut wire strung between the porch pillars. Like a piece of deli meat, the skin and tissues wobbled and dangled and then slid off, landing next to his head with a wet splat.

The door opened, and there was the sound of several feet crossing the porch. The first four belonged to the hound, who bounded up to him and sniffed his ravaged face cursorily before being booted off by another foot, this one belonging to the sick bastard who had done this to him.

The man stood over Combs, an awful, gleeful smile on his bearded face. His shoulders rose and fell quickly, and Combs realized that the man was chuckling. He just couldn't hear him over the rising of blood into his own ears.

The smiling lips moved, and the man spoke, but Combs couldn't make sense of any of it. He just raised the crossbow and pulled the trigger.

****

Clayton Morrell was, as always, awake well before the dawn.

He made coffee on Diggy Palmer's gas stove, which was smaller than his own but still worked alright in a pinch.

He had heard the shots the night before, two of them, and had waited anxiously for Slaterline to return and confirm that the complications had been taken care of. It had grown late, however, and the significant stresses of the day weighed heavily on Clayton's eyelids. He laid down and got his obligatory two hours, plus an extra one. He had absolute faith in Slaterline and imagined that he probably had taken some of the night to dispose of the body. Slaterline was good about things like that, which was precisely the reason that Clayton had gone out in search of a man like him.

He drank his coffee, ate some jerky, and dressed in the multiple layers of high-tech cold weather gear that would take him comfortably though a day on the steppes. With any luck at all, he would stain some of that expensive gear with grizzly blood before the day was out.

Clayton stepped out of the tent and into the breathtaking cold of the Alaskan pre-dawn. There was a dim light coming from Slaterline's tent, and Clayton smiled to himself and wondered what kind of terrific story his friend was going to tell him this morning. The kill before the kill. The necessary effort to vanquish all obstacles in the pursuit of the goal.

He walked to Slaterline's tent and unzipped the flap, ducked inside, and closed the flap behind him. Slaterline laid still and quiet on his cot, the sleeping bag pulled up to his hairline.

"Gets a little colder out here than in Botswana, eh, Slat?" Clayton said.

Slaterline continued to lie still, not even snoring. Clayton reached over and turned up the heat on the gas stove, grabbed Slaterline's arm, and shook it. The man was cold and stiff.

"What the hell?" Clayton said.

He pulled the sleeping bag away from Slaterline's face and gasped, gagged, staggered back, and nearly overturned the gas stove.

Slaterline's face had been removed from the eyebrows down, peeled off and removed with surgical skill. If it weren't for the little daggers on the neck of the corpse, Clayton would not have been able to tell it was him at all.

Clayton pulled himself together, got up, and moved back to the side of the cot. His predatory side kicked in— it was something he had practiced and cultivated over many years, a certain detachment that he believed allowed him to have great success in both business and big game hunting.

He forced himself to look at Slaterline as though he were just another carcass, another skinned-out mammal, ready to be packed in ice.

The process carried out on Slaterline's face was done with great precision and care, and that was enough to make Clayton fight a chill that came from more than the frigid morning. He continued to inspect the corpse and discovered a single puncture wound over the heart, crossed with thin incisions. It looked like an arrow had killed Slaterline.

Clayton was somewhat relieved that the removal of his face had not been the cause of Slaterline's demise, but the problem was not going away. The madman who wanted him dead was still at large and had now killed his best and most faithful guide.

How had he come and gone without being heard? Why hadn't he tried to kill Clayton while he was in the camp, moving about freely? He needed answers from the hired men, but he also needed to play it cool, or he would end up with a mutiny on his hands. He knew this much to be true; he had seen the fear in the eyes of Palmer and some of the other men, the ones who now constituted his entire party.

There would be no way to cover this up, no way to continue the hunt as though nothing had happened. But Clayton was unwilling to run. Retreat meant defeat, and this adversary wanted him to do exactly that. Clayton had not run from anyone in a long time, and his business motto was to defeat, destroy, and extract any valuable commodities. He planned to carry out this same mode of attack against this hillbilly.

Back through the flap and into the cold wind he went, seeing now that the east was turning pink and the wind was turning south, bringing more bone-chattering cold from the top of the world. The clearing was crosshatched with trails, all of them human. It looked as though a grand and elaborate dance had taken place while was sleeping. In the deep of the clearing, the wind erased the prints, and he could see where Slaterline had been dragged into his tent. The drag marks only began at the edge of the clearing, which meant he had been carried up to that point by something.

Other tracks led in the opposite direction, straight out into the steppe and onwards until they disappeared. Clayton went to the other tents and beat his gloves against the flaps, cursed with a calculated anger and called for the attention of his men.

The flaps opened and three sleepy faces peered out, looking worried, looking suspicious.

"Can anyone explain to me why no one was on watch last night?" Clayton asked. "Because I have some pretty irrefutable proof that no one was watching this camp at some point during the night."

The three heads bobbed around, and everyone looked at everyone else. It was clear that no one wanted to give an answer, given what they had just been told. Finally, Diggy Palmer spoke up.

"There were bears at the edge of camp last night," he said. "We heard 'em, and I set Scoundrel and Big Bob out to run 'em off. There's no bear hunting in the dark in Alaska or anywhere else I know of, but that doesn't mean you have to lay in your tent like a sausage and wait to get eaten. They didn't run 'em off too far, so we can go stalking at first light, like you wanted."

Clayton stood and listened to the story. He believed it. He could see bear tracks from where he stood, shining his flashlight around the edge of camp. What he couldn't figure was how the madman timed it so that he could drag Slaterline into his tent while the others were away spooking the bears off. Why hadn't he heard anything? Why had no one woken him up?

"You've been duped," he finally said. "Gear up and come on. I've got something to show you. Then, we have hunting to do."

The men didn't take well to the sight of the freshly skinned Slaterline, and Clayton had not imagined that they would. All the better. Scared and angry men worked well in the wild, while Clayton preferred the opposite for business. In business, calm and ice cold seemed to do the trick.

Clayton was in business mode whether he was in the boardroom or the bunker. He did not differentiate between killing beasts and making deals. Heads rolled everywhere he went, and he prided himself on his unflinching attitude.

But today, he needed savages. He needed pissed off souls who were so afraid for their lives that they would chew through their enemy and come out the other end spitting blood and smiling broadly. He could get them there. He could rile them and manipulate them. But in the end, he would be the one to put a big, fat bullet in Mr. Psychopathic Hillbilly. The only shame was that he wouldn't be able to hang the prick's head on his wall. Clayton was pretty sure there were serious laws against that sort of thing.

"I have brought you here to tell you: we are not taking this to the police," Clayton told the remaining guides. "Not yet at least. We have a responsibility to uphold. As men, as citizens, as red-blooded mammals with an instinct to survive. Do we not?"

The response that he received was less than enthusiastic, but he had expected that. This was merely a starting point, and these men were merely pieces that he would have to manipulate along the way. And that was easy enough.

"With poor Slaterline gone, you all stand to make one-hundred and twenty percent more on this expedition."

He registered their surprise—something he loved to do in all scenarios.

"Oh, it's true. Slat was my personal guide, and he was slated to gain a pretty penny on this trip. I write all of this off, so it doesn't matter to me where the money goes. What matters to me is if I have men with me. Men who are ready, willing, and able to climb over the next peak and take the next step. We have a battleground before us, gentlemen, and I am the general."

He looked around the tent. The three men that looked back at him seemed like they could not decide if he was the second coming of Christ or the devil himself. He made up their minds for them.

"Gentlemen. I am going to make you Alaska-rich beyond your wildest dreams. You'll be legends. Desperadoes. You can buy black hats and ride through old gold mining towns and steal their women, I really don't care. I'll pay for it all. But you have to do this one thing for me. You have to trudge through the damned snow and the damned cold and look out for the damned bears until I can track down the son of a bitch who killed my friend and kill him completely and entirely dead. Amen. Is everyone with me?"

That struck a chord with the three men. They signed up, got on board. The two who he didn't know even the names of introduced themselves to him.

Leonard Betts was a big man with a little head and very long, dirty fingernails. He said he was good with a knife and could trap any animal with feet and some without, which Clayton took to mean fish. Leonard carried a big Bowie knife on each hip, and a little stiletto knife in his boot. Clayton gave him a shotgun and said to start with that, to go to the knives if the guy was still breathing after a load of lead pellets to the chest.

The other remaining guide, besides Diggy Palmer, was a pitiful looking scrap of a kid that said his name was Keith Poot.

The name alone was enough to make somebody wonder where the hell this poor soul might end up, but here he was, in Alaska. And now, he was a top guide on a millionaire's bear hunt. Or maybe now it was a man hunt. Poot couldn't be sure, and he expressed his reservations loudly.

"I just want to let everyone here know that I do not approve of any man-hunting or any other sort of cannibalism or degradation of the human body," Poot said, his voice thin and pealing on the cold morning air.

Clayton was not moved by this appeal. It rang out like an empty request, just as the sun was coming up. Clayton put his hand on Keith Poot's shoulder and steered him aside; spoke to him in a fatherly tone.

"I know you, Poot," Clayton said. "I know you better than you know yourself. Do you know why?"

Poot shook his blonde, shaggy head.

"I know you because I have seen you in every office and every boardroom across the goddamn continent, even all the way around the world. Your type survives because they do what they are told, and then, they curl up like a little pill bug once things get beyond their comprehension. Do you know about the pill bug, Poot?"

Poot remembered some pill bugs fondly. It seemed like, when he was a little kid, they always rolled up into little round, brown balls when threatened. But now that he was grown, he couldn't get them to curl up anymore. When he tried, they just crunched between his fingers, like undercooked beans.

"I know what a pill bug is, sir," Poot managed. "Little guy that curls up when he's scared of something."

Clayton gave Poot his best look of approval. It was a little dance of the face, and it had to end with one eyebrow raised.

"That's exactly right, Poot," he said. "Now, are you going to do what you are told and then curl up like a pitiful bug? Or are you going to do what you *have to do* and then walk down this mountain like a goddamn hero?"

Poot stood there, straight up like a beanpole. He didn't have any idea how to please people like Mr. Clayton. But he did know bears, and he thought that knowledge might be his saving grace in this situation.

"I got you, Mr. Clayton," Poot said. "Don't worry about me. I'm all in."

Clayton was pleased to know that he still had three men on his side. Three dispensable men. One seemed to be an able guide but was too easily rattled. One was a pinheaded giant with a penchant for blades, and the last was a toe-headed simpleton that shirked against the idea of killing men.

The three of them combined would not equal one Slaterline, but Clayton had no choice but to work with what he had. In the growing pinkness of an Alaskan morning, each man tried to ignore the beauty of the dawn as they readied their various weapons. The dawn wrought such beauty, but the day was apt to bring so much bloodshed.

Combs couldn't see so well anymore. One of his eyes had been sheared by the razor wire. But beyond that, his new mask was a cumbersome accoutrement. The eye holes jostled around, and the chin wouldn't hold in place. Plus, the whole thing stank like a dead man.

"What a night," Combs said. "What a goddamn night."

He was resting, and he mumbled some tortured words and bled his life blood into the fur and chest of his best friend and closest confidant. The hound didn't even come in at a close second. The dog hadn't even come back last night. Combs wept now into the bosom of wrath. The breadth of the night.

****

It was necessary to take the long way around, everyone knew that to be true. Not a man in the party would have willingly followed that path that Slaterline took to the cabin in the woods, that trail of doom and gore.

They hiked east in the pale light of the morning and gave a wide berth to the river valley, fording the brown waters in one place where a massive fir had fallen across the banks. They would find another crossing later, closer to the cabin, Clayton explained. For now, the river was their friend, as it provided an ample barrier between them and the turf of their enemy.

The snow was deep, and the going was tough, but by mid-morning, they crested a rise and caught a faint whiff of wood smoke. Indeed, in the western distance, back across the river, a thin trail of white was twisting lazily up into the cold sky.

"We're getting close now," Clayton said, his voice barely above a whisper. "So, from this point on, no more speaking. Hand signals only. Got it?"

Palmer and Betts gave him a thumbs up. Poot blurted, "Got it," and then blushed red when the other three men scowled at him.

They crept down the riverbank and found a shallow crossing where they were able to ford the waters by hopping from rock to rock. Once across, Clayton then pointed to each man in turn and gestured to various parts of the woods around them, indicating that he wanted them to split up and approach the cabin from various angles.

Combs had not slept, but he felt as though he had dreamed. And in his dreams, he was spoken to by a great and terrible bear, but he was not afraid. The bear told him that he would be victorious because of his loyalty to his friends and his protection of the land. The bear in the dream then told him to get up, to make preparations for the day. And that was what Rodney Combs did.

With his long strides and mindless energy, Betts came within sight of the cabin before the others and drew his blades before he approached. He sniffed the air: woodsmoke, evergreens, the sharp scent of cold, as well as something deep and rank and alive, the smell of big game. But there was something else, too, and the scent grew stronger as he came to the edge of the tree line and considered the clearing in which the cabin stood.

It smelled like fuel oil.

In the instant that the thought crossed his mind, there was a flicker and a spark in the crawlspace beneath the cabin. Something flared to life, and Betts thought that he had seen a terrible, ghastly face in the gloom. In the next moment, there was a sharp click, and a flaming arrow whizzed out of the dark hole and headed in his direction.

Betts never moved his feet. He could tell almost immediately that the shot would miss him. It was aimed low and to his left, and the arrow struck the base of a cedar tree. In an instant, the tree burst into flames. The fire raced up the trunk, crackling and consuming with voracious power, but it also spread out across the snow arcing through the drifts, meeting other trees that also went up like dried kindling.

The dancing flames encircled the place where Betts was standing, dumbstruck, and proceeded to close in on him with horrible speed. He tried to run, but he slipped in the rapidly melting snow and ice. The earth was so wet, and his nostrils were filled with the smell of fuel. It was on his gloves, soaking into his pants and parka.

Like a pack of wolves, the fire was upon him, leaping and climbing up his back. He rose and fell again, screaming in pain. A flock of birds burst from a tree, cackling into the sky as though carried aloft by the sounds of a man in agony.

Betts tried to roll, to suffocate the flames, but he laid in a pool of accelerant, and he thrashed about in an atmosphere of vapors. His screams grew weaker and weaker, which soon turned into whimpers and cries before he finally fell silent. His knives laid steaming at his sides, their blades heated and tempered, purpled by the flames.

Moving carefully through a hallow, Clayton heard the screams in the near distance. It didn't sound like Palmer. Too deep to be Poot. He wondered what fate had befallen Betts and how such a brute of a man could fall so quickly.

He felt the urge to move faster to close ground on the cabin while the lunatic was occupied with the big man, but he knew this decision would be unwise, and he resisted the impulse. Every beast he had ever killed, he did so with patience.

Diggy Palmer had seen the whole thing. He had prowled around to the far end of the clearing, slung his rifle over his shoulder, and climbed a tree. Palmer had no intention of walking right up to a cabin where an obviously deranged individual was lying in wait.

From his spot among the branches, he had seen Betts approach, knives drawn. He watched the big man come through the woods, looking like a Sasquatch or some other mythical beast. He stopped to look around, and then, the world around him burst into flames. Palmer couldn't believe what he was seeing, and he was completely and totally transfixed by the moment.

The flames, the screams, the birds, the tiny curl of acrid

smoke that finally defeated what had been a large and powerful man only moments before.

Had Palmer not been so absorbed in watching Betts burn to death, he might have seen movement within the cabin. He might have noticed someone slipping past the narrow window. And he might have noticed when the loft door, high under the peak of the cabin roof, opened just a crack.

But because he had been so distracted by the action across the clearing, the first thing he did notice was when some mangled freak in a Halloween mask threw open the loft door and hurled a hatchet directly at him. Palmer shifted on the tree limb, panicked, his eyes tracing the flight of the blade and handle as it turned in the air. He was about to leap from the tree, but he had come to this conclusion too slowly. The blade cut through the meat of his ankle, shattered the bone and severed the tendons, finally sinking into the bark of the tree with a dull thud.

Palmer was shocked at the sound of his own screams. They came from a place of such deep anguish. He nearly toppled to the ground but managed to turn his body in time to hug the trunk of the tree with both arms.

His eyes squeezed tightly closed. The rough bark of the tree pressed against one cheek while the cold steel of his rifle barrel touched the other. With great effort, Palmer managed to stop screaming, to slow his breathing. His leg had already gone numb, and he could hear the dripping of his own steadily flowing blood as it spattered down onto the snow below.

And then, the tree moved. It was a subtle movement, a swaying like when the wind blew, but the air was still. The tree swayed again, and his limb bobbed slightly.

Something grunted below him.

Palmer forced himself to open his eyes, and when he did, he looked down into the angry, yellow eyes of a massive bear. The bear started up the tree toward him, its long and curving claws grappling with the bark, finding purchase, pulling its massive body ever upward.

With a gasp and a curse, Palmer released the trunk and swung his rifle around from his back, instantly and expertly taking aim at the grizzly below. His draw was fluid and quick, but the shock of seeing the bear had caused him to forget that he was lacking a foot, and Palmer tottered and fell from that high perch. He landed on his neck, and the sharp crack that resonated through the clearing surprised even the bear.

Clayton had come out of the hollow in time to see Palmer fall from the tree. He crouched in the shadow of an ancient alder and watched as the grizzly shimmied back down the trunk and commenced to nibble on Palmer's ears and nose.

The numbers were changing too quickly, and his advantage was being decimated. It was now just two men to one. Normally, he wouldn't hate those odds. The problem was, it seemed that his enemy had some friends on this mountain that he had not taken into account.

Poot had managed to slip up to the cabin while the bear was headed up the tree after Palmer. He did not see Palmer fall, but he knew from what he did see that Palmer was a dead man, one way or another. No sense in wasting bullets to save a dead man.

He was surprised to find the back door unlocked, and he moved inside soundlessly, easing the door closed behind him. He crouched and listened in the semi-darkness, heard nothing, but he knew that the man they were after had to be in here somewhere.

He had his rifle at the ready, safety switched off, one in the chamber.

Silence.

Poot moved slowly through the cabin, testing boards with the toe of his boot, trying to avoid ones that would squeak or creak and betray his position. It was dark enough to conceal a man in the shadows, but it was too quiet to attack without giving something away, and Poot figured he would have to rely on his ears.

There was a soft sound from above, the slightest clunk from the loft. It came again, near the front of the cabin, and Poot carefully, patiently, made his way toward it, gun barrel pointed toward the ceiling.

His ears told him where to go, and he went precisely to where Combs wanted him to go. It was quite dark. What grim, gray light there was could conceal a lot. Poot never saw the loop of wire that hung right before his face, and when it first touched his neck, he thought it was nothing more than a cobweb.

When Combs yanked on the other end of the wire from his place in the loft, he lifted Poot clean off of his feet. The sharp metal sawed through the heavy leather gloves that Combs wore cut into his skin, but he held fast and leaned back, pulling upward, his face red with exertion.

Poot did not scream. Could not scream. The only sounds from below Combs's feet were some soft gagging, wrenching sounds and the flapping, fabric sounds of Poot flailing his legs helplessly. Poot did not hang there long, only a few seconds. And then, there was a loud thump, followed by a smaller, harder one, and Combs relaxed. He winced as he unwound the wire that had embedded itself in his fingers and palms. He worked off the leather gloves and left it all in a bloody pile on the loft floor.

Unless he had lost count, there would only be one more, and that one was the trophy he had been waiting for.

****

Clayton laid on his stomach in the snow, sixty yards away from the cabin's front door. He waited. He waited for Poot to flush the man out, or for the lunatic to flush Poot out. He waited to hear shots, or screams, or to see more flames.

At this point, he figured that nothing could surprise him.

He laid in wait, but there was nothing but the birds singing in the trees. The bear that had been chewing on dead, old Diggy Palmer. had lost interest and disappeared into the forest. The sky had clouded over, and it began to snow.

And then, the front door opened, and Douglas Slaterline walked out onto the porch. Only it wasn't Slaterline, not quite. His eyes were empty, hollow sockets, shriveled at the edges. His mouth hung crooked and gaping, his lips white.

"Dear God," Clayton whispered, staring through the scope in disbelief. "The psycho is wearing Slat's face."

It was as much diversion as Combs needed. If not for that mask, Clayton would have pulled the trigger as soon as he walked out that door, sniped him dead right there on the front porch with a neat hole between his eyes. But he didn't, and Combs raised a shotgun and peppered the brush with buckshot.

Clayton snarled as he felt the little sharp scraps of metal pierce the skin of his cheek and tear at his parka. One caught him on the knuckle of his trigger finger, and he cursed and shook that hand.

Combs let it fly with the other barrel, but Clayton had rolled behind a tree stump and was spared any further damage. He listened now as the man on the porch wearing the face of his friend cracked open the breach to reload. He took advantage of the pause and took aim, leveling his rifle over the stump. He took a breath and squeezed the trigger with his bloodied finger. The shot was just wide of center mass, took a chunk of Combs's shirt and a bit of his rib meat. He went down squalling and scooted himself back into the door of the cabin.

Clayton was on his feet and running. He fired a shot from his hip and missed, splintering the edge of the door frame just as Combs was kicking the door closed. Clayton mounted the porch steps at full speed and crashed through the door with a shout.

Combs had been ready for that. He was tucked off to the side of the door with his shotgun still empty, but he slashed at Clayton's legs with a long-bladed hunting knife as he came through the door. Blood painted the wooden floor in long arcs, and Clayton fell, crashing into the wooden table, turning over a chair. He scrambled to right himself, to get hold of his rifle and turn to defend himself, but when he looked, Combs was no longer by the door. He seemed to have vanished like a mist.

Something bumped against Clayton's knee. He looked down and stared into Poot's bulging and bloodshot eyes. The rest of the boy's body was slumped in an awkward posture a few feet away in a widening lake of dark blood.

He forced himself to look away from the awful scene and scanned the room for Combs, his finger twitching on the trigger of his rifle. The cabin was not large; there were not many places for a grown man to hide. Then, he saw the bloody footprints heading out the front door. The coward had run.

Just as Clayton struggled to his feet and braced himself

against the pain in his cut leg, preparing to make pursuit, the back door of the cabin burst open, and the man charged in, wielding an axe. He closed in quickly on Clayton, who turned and raised his rifle to fire, only to have it slammed from his hands by the bit of the axe. The rifle clattered to the floor and skidded across the room, coming to rest beneath a bookcase.

Combs raised the axe again and came down with it, screaming with effort and rage. Clayton staggered back and felt a breeze as the blade narrowly missed his face. Combs's mask was falling off, showing half of his real face, the other side still obscured by the butchered and gory visage of Douglas Slaterline.

He kept coming, swinging the axe wildly, shattering dishes and picture frames, splintering chairs and demolishing light fixtures in his wild attempts to cleave Clayton in half. As he swung, he spoke in a choked voice that sounded almost as though he were pleading with Clayton. It was like a prayer or a confession, and the words were hard to make out.

"My. Friends. You. Can't. Take."

He spoke in rhythm with his attack, surely nonsensical ramblings from deep within a troubled soul.

"No. Right. No. Right."

He swung down hard and missed the scrambling Clayton once again, and this time, the axe stuck fast in the wooden floorboards. Clayton saw his chance and ran at Combs, leapt and kicked him square in the chest. The blow sent him staggering backward until he hit the wall at the other end of the room and slumped to the floor among the shattered artifacts of his lonely life.

Combs made no move to get up, and Clayton allowed himself a moment to catch his breath before moving to the bookshelf to retrieve his rifle. He checked the breach; he only needed one round. Then, he reconsidered.

"You know," Clayton said, looking askance at Combs. "I think a bullet might be too easy a way out for you. But still, I want you to feel this, just once."

He sighted quickly and fired one shot into Combs's stomach. The man bellowed and writhed, tore the flesh mask from his face and coughed blood out onto his chest.

"That one was for me," Clayton said.

Then, he stepped forward and pulled the axe from the floor. He tested its edge with his thumb.

"Still sharp," he said, as though to himself. "Now, what I'm going to do with this will be for my friend that you cut up."

He leveled a look at Combs, who regarded him through calm and hooded eyes; he looked as if he might pass out soon, and Clayton did not intend to let him blackout without feeling a little more hell first.

Clayton stepped forward and spun the axe in his hands, sneering, death in his eyes. And then, the floor exploded beneath him.

In an eruption of splinters and boards, hinges and hasps, a trap door in the floor gave way to a force that burst upwards from somewhere in the darkness below the cabin. A mountain of fur and teeth and black claws rose up before him, blocking out Combs, blocking out the rest of the room, blocking out any thought in Clayton's head.

The grizzly that came up roaring through the floor stood ten feet tall and had its powerful arms open wide as though to crush the world in its grasp. Clayton went cold, glanced once at the rifle where he had set it down, and moved. He had not even made it one step when the mountain of muscle and fury and bloodlust fell upon him, and the last thing Clayton Morrell ever knew was that he was not going to get his bear.

****

The sun was going down over the mountains, and the sky was a mural of purples, oranges, and reds. It had snowed all afternoon and into the evening, and the fresh powder covered all traces of what had happened that day.

The body of Rodney Combs laid in repose by the river's edge. It was placed there by his best friend, right after Rodney had died, right after his friend had killed the bad man. All evening, more and more friends came down from the mountains and in off the steppe. They came to see the body of their friend, and they all cried in their own animalistic way.

The bodies of the other men were taken apart and shared. Their bones were scattered. But Rodney Combs remained whole, and his body stayed by the river to this day.

STEPHEN R. KING

Copyright © 2017 by Stephen King

This book is a work of fiction. Any references to historical events, real people, or real places are used fictitiously. Other names, characters, places, and events are products of the author's imagination, and any resemblance to actual events or places or person, living or dead, is entirely coincidental.

All rights reserved, including the right to reproduce this book or portions thereof in any form whatsoever.

Manufactured in the United States of America
Designed by Magic Pen Designs

Printed in Great Britain
by Amazon

df86f4f6-6ef3-424a-8be3-70d886990f67R01